Lt. Dan, a lieutenant sheriff, and Dr. Jacob, an educator, are accidentally thrown together. There are four major conferences scheduled in the city, and because of that, there are no hotel rooms for miles around. Sharing is the only option.

The two men come from different backgrounds and face difficulties that make their lives complicated. Against all odds, can they overcome the obstacles and build a lasting relationship?

Love Comes After Fifty
Copyright © 2023 James J Gregoryk
ISBN: 978-1-4874-3877-7
Cover art by Tyffani Lyons

Published by eXtasy Books Inc

Look for us online at:
www.eXtasybooks.com

Love Comes After Fifty
The Cop and the Teacher

By

James J Gregoryk

DEDICATION

To my friends and family that never stopped believing in me. A special thank you to Jerry, Annika, Devin, Tom, Frank and Robert. In Memory of Metka H. and Robert L. Hansen

CHAPTER ONE

Jacob arrived at his hotel in Athens, Georgia. He was there to attend a conference for his school system. The noise from the chatter between customers and staff drifted through the foyer. A large sign at the desk stated the entire hotel had been fully booked long ago, and people left clearly disappointed as they hurried away in search of other accommodation, commenting as they went about how they should've booked months ago. Jacob sidled up to the counter and started to check in.

As they confirmed his room reservation, the clerk quietly asked, "Mr. Easton, you've booked a room with two queen-size beds, and I see that you only have one set of luggage. Are you expecting anyone to join you?"

Surprised by the question, Jacob answered, "No, when I called for a reservation, that was all you had open, but I took it anyway. Why?"

"Sir, we have a police officer that needs a room. It seems he's some sort of VIP. We even got phone calls from the Chief of Police and the Sheriff asking us to try and help him out. We'd make it well worth your while if you'd consider sharing your room with him. Currently there are four huge conferences happening this week, so everyone's having difficulty finding a room."

The young man was very dramatic as he explained the situation.

Jacob pretended a cough to cover up his amusement over the theatrics. He noticed people standing around him, looking to be waiting for his answer.

1

Pausing for a second and looking the manager in the eye, Jacob took a deep breath, smiled, and said, "A VIP policeman? The idea of saving some money is piquing my curiosity, and I like the idea of helping out an officer of the law. I guess it can't hurt to see what you mean. How much, and who?"

The clerk showed Jacob the discount, fifty percent off the price of his room.

Jacob's smile lit his face up. "I like the how much. Now, who needs to be answered."

The clerk pointed his index finger to the parking lot.

Jacob scanned the area where the clerk seemed to be indicating. A man came into Jacob's vision. The guy stood outside by a black car. Jacob's eyes widened as he saw a poorly dressed man in a wrinkled, dirty-looking, and ill-fitted suit. Jacob noticed that the man could not possibly button the jacket because his huge stomach was in the way. Jacob's focus turned from that man to the clerk. "You've got to be kidding me. You expect me to share my room with him?" Jacob looked back directly at the disheveled-looking man.

The clerked followed Jacob's gaze and shook his head. "No, no, no, not *Jabba the Hutt* . . . him," he said and pointed slightly farther to the left.

Jacob spotted another man who stood a short distance from Mr. *Jabba*. His breath caught for a second, and he stared in disbelief. His shirt collar suddenly felt too tight. Jacob wiped his now sweaty palms on his pants. There stood a man dressed in a perfectly fitted police uniform who was just too beautiful to be real. At least six feet four inches tall and built like a god. He had gorgeous deep blue eyes. Curly short black hair, a strong jawline, dimpled cheeks, and a perfect nose made his masculine face look like a movie star's. But it was when he smiled that Jacob lost his breath, a smile that just might have the ability to kill people. Jacob mouthed *Wow*. Even from this distance, Jacob could see his sparkling blue eyes dancing with anticipation and looking hopeful for a positive answer. A dreamy mood came over Jacob.

"Well, what do you think?" the clerk asked, snapping him back to reality.

Jacob glanced back at that handsome godlike man and mopped the sweat from his forehead as concern flowed through him. "Just look at him. I'm going to bet this won't work at all. He's the epitome of the straight redneck." Jacob was sure he'd heard several disappointing *aahs* from people around him. Jacob paused for a moment. His attention was refocused on the police officer. He straightened up, checked his clothes, and ran his fingers through his hair to see if it was still in place. He returned to the fidgeting clerk. Finally, he said, "Well, maybe him, but I get to decide after meeting him."

The clerk fist pumped in the air and said, "Yes! I'll get the manager and then have him retrieve the gentleman for you to meet him. The poor man's desperate for a place to sleep. It seems every room in town's booked."

Jacob squeaked out, "Okay."

The clerk informed the manager of the situation. The manager shook Jacob's hand and then practically pranced out the door to escort the policeman to Jacob.

Mumbling to himself, Jacob concluded, "If you put chiffon wings on that man, he'd fly."

The young clerk behind the check-in desk barked out a laugh, and only then did Jacob realize he'd said that out loud.

The manager talked to the officer and pointed. The officer looked in the direction that the manager was pointing. He surfed through the crowd but stopped when his attention locked onto Jacob.

Jacob mumbled to himself, "What the hell am I thinking? Am I really going to share my room with a stranger? Yep, I'm getting senile. I swear that would be the only explanation of what's happening to me." He suddenly realized he'd forgotten himself and mumbled that all out loud, and his face flushed

Now looking his way, the clerk said, "Sir, are you okay? Can I get you anything?"

Nearly begging, Jacob replied, "I could use a *Diet Coke*." Suddenly there it appeared on a silver platter. Jacob smiled and thanked the clerk. Opening the soda and taking a swallow, he said, "I could get used to this special treatment."

Officer I'm-Too-Sexy-For-This-Uniform moved quickly through the doors focused entirely on Jacob as he walked straight up to him. The manager acted like a giggly twelve-year-old girl and followed right behind.

Jacob's disapproving look caught the manager's attention, so he calmed himself.

In an overly excited voice, the manager extended his palm toward Jacob and introduced them. "Dr. Jacob Easton, this is Lieutenant Daniel Winters. Dan, this is Jake. Jake, this is Dan." He moved his open palm, flipping back and forth during the introductions.

Whipping an icy glare at the manager, Jacob said, "My name is Jacob." He took another sip of his drink. The manager stepped quietly back.

Officer I-Am-Just-Too-Sexy's smile broadened and his eyes sparkled, causing Jacob to nearly choke on his drink.

His face flushed bright red for a moment, but then taking a deep breath, Jacob pulled himself together. Jacob retorted in his finest Forrest Gump imitation, "It's my pleasure to meet you, Lieutenant Dan."

As the lieutenant stared deadpan straight into Jacob's eyes, his smile broadened even more, and then the most beautiful, rich laughter rolled out of him. His laughter was contagious as it floated around the room, causing people around him to laugh, too.

"I'll be damned. It's nice to meet you, too, Forrest," Lieutenant Dan replied cheerfully.

Jacob just about melted. He breathed out heavily, and his smile seemed to wobble. This lasted only a second.

Dan reached out his hand and shook Jacob's. "May I say, I'm going to be eternally grateful. If you hadn't been so kind as to consider sharing your room with me, I would've had to share a bed with *Jabba the Hutt* out there."

A fine mist of *Diet Coke* came spewing out of Jacob's mouth, and the manager caught most of it. Jacob apologized to the poor man over and over. Turning and facing Lieutenant Dan. "This is your fault, Lieutenant."

"Agreed." Dan snapped to attention and saluted.

Jacob smiled. "Okay, then, I guess we should get checked in."

Lieutenant Dan gave Jacob a smile that could make the strongest of men weak-kneed, and the two proceeded to finalize their check in.

"This is my luggage," Jacob said, informing the porter and pointing to his bags. He looked around. He turned to Lieutenant Dan, saw just one bag, and asked, "Is that all the luggage you have?"

"Yeah, just this one bag," Dan told him.

Jacob laughed, as he had four bags in all.

Jacob glanced back at *Jabba* as they started to follow the porter. He laughed to himself at the fact that everyone had called that man *Jabba the Hut*

"Dude, you should stop laughing now. You saved me from having to put up with the *Jabba* by doing this, and I appreciate it more than I can tell you." Dan smiled his wonderful, heart-melting smile.

Jacob stared at this gorgeous man for a second and then shook it off. Clearing his throat, he said, "With that charming smile and your dancing dark blue eyes, you might just mesmerize everyone. So could you turn it all off, please? I don't want them to start following us around."

Dan just playfully winked at Jacob.

Arriving at their room, the porter opened the door. The pastel-painted and nicely furnished room opened to a huge sitting area. Canvasing the rest of the room, Jacob became alarmed to find only a king-size bed at the far end of the room.

"Wait!" Jacob snapped, and the porter stopped in the middle of a heavy suitcase lift. Jacob continued, "This is the wrong room. Our room has two queen-size beds, so this isn't it!"

Lieutenant Dan nodded his head in agreement.

The porter said, "I'm sorry, but they remodeled some of the rooms recently, and this must've been one of them. Let me get the manager."

After a few moments, the manager tapped on the open door, walked into the room, and flamboyantly announced, "Oh my, this room's one that we redecorated. Either you can still share it for a larger discount, or the officer will have to go elsewhere." His pleading gaze bounced from Jacob to Lieutenant Dan, continuing back and forth and back and forth as he anxiously waited for a response.

Gently taking Jacob's arm and moving him slightly aside, Dan looked directly into his eyes and spoke quietly, "Look, Jacob, I know this is a lot to ask, but I got to Athens at four-fifteen this morning. There's nothing for miles around. The person that was supposed to make the reservations for me got the dates mixed up. I promise to be on my very best law enforcement behavior. I'll pay for the entire room. Please consider it!"

Dan again turned on his wonderful smile, but he added pleading puppy dog eyes. Finally, Jacob spoke. "Your very best behavior . . . you promise?"

Dan lifted his right hand and vowed, "I swear it. I'll be a

total gentleman at all times. I won't even fart in bed."

"That farting in bed stuff must be a total cop thing to say." Jacob gave him the stink-eye look.

Lieutenant Dan made big puppy dog eyes at Jacob. He then turned on that wonderful smile.

Jacob caved. "Okay! However, you'd better keep your word, or you're out on your rear end."

Jacob immediately busied himself, took his things out of his suitcases, hung things up and put away his folded clothes into the drawers, He placed his toiletries in the bathroom.

Lieutenant Dan's phone rang as soon as they closed the door to the room, and he answered it. He sounded like the man in charge. "Officer Mallory's a professional sheriff's deputy, and I'm sure he acted appropriately with the entire situation. No, that's my only comment at this time." He hung up. "Shit, that's all I need with the sheriff on maternity leave and me here."

"What's wrong?"

"Just some difficulty back at the Sheriff's Office. I need to see if this has hit the news yet." He sat down and turned on the TV.

"Aren't you going to unpack your stuff?"

"Nah, I'll just leave it in the suitcase and take stuff out as I need it. Right now, I need to see how the news is reporting this situation," Dan replied, but his focus never left the TV as he flipped through the channels.

Teacher Jacob flashed to the surface. "You most certainly will unpack and hang stuff up, or it'll be too wrinkled to wear anyplace. Your wife might not take it well if you appeared everywhere looking like you slept in your clothes!" With his hands on his hips and a glare that could stop traffic, Jacob made it clear what Dan needed to do.

Quick as a wink, Dan popped off the bed, saluted, and began hanging up his shirts and pants and other stuff and then, standing like a scolded boy, said to Jacob, "May I just leave my socks, t-shirts, and underwear in my suitcase, Mom?" A warm, teasing smile broke across Dan's face, making Jacob shake his head and chuckle. Dan cleared his throat. "And so, we're clear on the subject. There's no Mrs. Winters. other than my mama and sisters-in-law, in my life." He winked playfully at Jacob.

Dan's playfulness made Jacob smile. "Dan, I'll bet you're like this all the time, not just with me, or you wouldn't be so playful with a stranger."

Dan winked again at Jacob. "How about you? Is there a Mrs. Forrest Gump?" Dan asked.

Pausing for a second, Jacob flat out told him, "Nope. I'm not into women because I'm gay. Do you have a problem with that?"

"Same here." With no emphasis or expression, Dan returned to watching the news.

Jacob stood open-mouthed as he stared at Dan.

His standing there gaping got Dan's attention. He retorted, "What? School teachers cornered the market on gay? Got news for you, bud . . . we're everywhere." Lieutenant Dan's killer smile brought the matter to a close. Then with twinkling eyes, he added, "Oh yeah? I'll try and remember to keep my hands off you while we're in bed." Again, returning to the TV when he finished, Dan refocused on what was on the set.

Jacob's face reddened, and he shook his finger at Dan. "You promised to be on your best policeman behavior," he said, raising his hand like Dan did when he swore earlier.

"I'll try and remember to do that, too," Dan side-mouthed without taking his attention away from the TV.

With hands on his hips, Jacob used his teacher's voice. "You try anything, and I'll slap the stupid right out of you."

Pausing the program, Dan put down the remote, stood to his full height, turned, and faced Jacob, whom he examined up and down.

Jacob's superior smirk faded.

"What are you, like five foot-five, maybe one hundred ten pounds? What are you going to do? Take me out with your cuteness?" Suddenly, Dan's hysterical laughter filled the air.

Jacob looked around and then to the door. He hoped people hadn't heard the peals of laughter in the hallway.

Dan's tears began rolling down his cheeks as his laughter filled the hotel room.

"I'll have you know I'm five-seven and a half and one hundred and thirty-two pounds, and I don't appreciate your — God, I just turned into some naggy old woman." Jacob had caught on that Dan was jerking his chain. He joined Dan's contagious laughter. It subsided as quickly as it started.

Dan straightened up, and he became serious. "Get cleaned up, Mr. Tough Man. I'm taking you out to dinner for letting me share this place with you. No arguing. Just do it." Dan stated as he took on the I'm-in-charge attitude.

"Yes, sir." Jacob saluted and headed into the bathroom. As he entered, he was muttering, "Why the hell am I so damned nervous, and why am I swearing like this? I never do. Now, why am I talking to myself?"

"I don't know," Dan said, clucking, "Why are you?"

Still staring at Jacob, Dan kept a silly smirk on his face.

Jacob's expression immediately changed to shit-I-said-that–out-loud as he stepped into the bathroom and closed the door.

Jacob brushed his teeth, changed his clothes, and combed his hair. He checked himself in the mirror from head to toe. "You're looking pretty good," he said to his reflection in the mirror. He smiled and opened the door.

Stepping out of the bathroom, Jacob froze. Dan had changed into blue jeans and a plaid shirt, looking ready for his modeling photoshoot in a sports magazine.

Dan mouthed *wow*. "Holy shit, Forrest, you clean up real good. You look totally hot. Remind me to talk to you about that ugly tie and sweater you had on earlier."

That certainly grabbed Jacob's attention. He looked down at what he had on and glanced in the full-length mirror. "I look okay, don't I?" The ogling look on Dan's face made him smile.

Changing the subject to the clothes Dan had just mentioned, Jacob said, "I love that bow tie I was wearing."

Straightening his folded-back shirt cuffs, Dan didn't even look up at Jacob. "Makes you look nerdy and old."

Pausing for a moment and then in a serious tone, Jacob stated, "Now let's set some guidelines so we've some clarity here. That way, we don't cross over each other's boundaries. Okay? First, you're way too young for me, and I'm too old for you."

Shutting off the television, Dan turned and looked at Jacob and raised one eyebrow, giving Jacob a look that said, "What on earth are you talking about?

Jacob decided to be blunt. "What are you? Maybe forty-five, if not younger, and I'm nearly sixty years old, almost old enough to be your father. We shouldn't get too friendly and keep this a business arrangement only. Don't you agree?"

Dan paused, put his hands on his knees and rose to his full height. "Damn, Jacob, what put your panties in a knot? First of all, I'm a month away from fifty-five, so we aren't that far apart in age. Second, I wasn't planning on asking you to marry me this evening, maybe tomorrow, depending on how the evening progresses, but not *this* evening." Getting his point across, Dan flashed his body-wilting smile. "And I'll make no promises about keeping any boundaries, so pull that stick out of your ass, and let's go have a nice dinner." Jacob gaped and stared until Dan said, "That gaping look isn't very attractive; I would lose it if I were you." Again, Dan turned on that smile of his.

"*Kay*," Jacob squeaked out.

Lieutenant Dan burst into laughter again, making Jacob laugh at himself, too. Gently leading Jacob to the door, Dan opened it and held it for Jacob, and off they went to dinner.

Chapter Two

Dan led the way into the hotel restaurant. Jacob worriedly looked around. "Dan, it looks like we'll have to wait for a table, which might be very long. You think it's worth it?"

Dan smiled and then went to the maître d' and spoke with him.

"Right this way, gentlemen," the maître d' indicated and led the way to the coziest table in the whole place. Again, Jacob looked surprised at Dan as they walked to the table.

Dan picked up on Jacob's perplexed look. "What? I made reservations."

"What could I get you gentlemen to drink?" the maître d' asked.

Dan answered, "I'll have double bourbon on the rocks with a twist. Wild Turkey if you have it, and you, Forrest?"

Blushing at the nickname, Jacob replied, "A glass of Chardonnay, please."

"Thank you, gentlemen. Your waiter, Chris, will bring them right up." He turned and left.

"What the fuck kind of drink is that?" Dan asked loud enough to be heard by anyone sitting nearby.

"Shhhhhh, it was what I wanted, besides I don't do well with the hard stuff," Jacob whispered.

"Ahhhh, *tequila makes your clothes come off,*" Dan sang out loud. Jacob hushed him and made a face at Dan like he was nuts. "I fu . . . fricken swear it's a song." Dan tried hard to defend himself but finally crossed his eyes and winked.

Jacob burst into laughter at Dan's goofy expression and

then replied. "No, nothing that risqué. I tend to throw up."

"Ewwww, barf breath, gross," Dan said, and they laughed.

The waiter came flittering over with their drinks. "Ooooh, I bet the big beefy guy gets the hard stuff," he said, all flirty and sassy to Dan. "And you . . ." His demeanor changed instantly to snotty as he rolled his eyes and placed the wine in front of Jacob, and then he snarked, "Get the wine."

That little fruitcake's snottiness crawled all over Jacob, yet keeping himself composed, he said, "And if you expect a tip, you'd better wipe that snotty expression off your face. Also, I would knock off the wisecracks and do your job!"

The waiter straightened up, nodded, and took off.

Dan nearly rolled in the aisle with laughter. It was that funny moment that lifted any awkward stiffness between them.

"Now that you straightened him out, little Jacob, tell me about yourself. Where are you from originally? Where do you teach? Your family and stuff like that?"

"First, how did you know I was in education?" Jacob asked.

Dan smiled and said, "With that stupid bow tie and cardigan sweater you had on, that was a dead giveaway. Plus, you're so damn bossy. You had to be an educator or a judge. Now back to my original questions."

Jacob began his story. "I was born in Charlotte, North Carolina, and grew up there with my four sisters and parents. I was the baby. I went to university here in Athens because they offered me an academic scholarship. I got my BS in Early Childhood Education and added my Masters in Special Education a couple of years later. My doctorate in Education Administration came next. I've worked in the same school system my entire career. My family's had nothing to do with me since I came out to them when I turned twenty. I haven't spoken to or had contact with most of them. Any communication

I've had has been through attorneys or my niece. I've got to say that's okay with me, as they were never very nice people. They only ever cared about having money and prestige. I guess about twenty years ago, when it was popular and almost prestigious to have a gay member in the family, my oldest sister called and left me a long message about how insensitive I was for not trying to keep contact with the family." Dan's eyes widened, and Jacob replied, "Yeah, I know. After they disowned me, it was suddenly my fault. I'm pretty sure it was more like she ran out of money and wanted mine. I never responded." Jacob blushed at his rambling mouth. "Wow, this wine's making my mouth run away with itself. How about you, Dan? Tell me about you."

"Jacob, you amaze me. I'm guessing you live alone and have your own home."

Jacob answered, "I don't live alone. I have two giant Siamese cats, Si and Amy. Amy will have kittens in about five weeks. I've a teacup poodle named Meme, who's also in the family way. Not that I wanted it that way, but it happened. God, that comes across so incredibly gay. I guess I've become the old spinster schoolmarm." Jacob laughed at himself, and Dan joined him.

"I'm glad you're comfortable telling me your life's story. It's like we've known each other for a long time. You're just so open and honest. I love that." Dan reached across the table and squeezed Jacob's hand.

The waiter reappeared. "Have you decided on an appetizer?" Again with the nasty attitude, his eyes nearly bugged out of his head when he spied Dan's hand placed on top of Jacob's.

Growling sounds came from Dan, and he said to the waiter, "Listen here, little Miss Snip and Snap, why don't you find someone that wants to wait on us?"

The maître d' appeared and asked, "Is there a problem

here?" His furrowed brows and a slight frown showed his concern.

"There wouldn't be if Chrissy here would do his or her job and mind his or her own goddamn business." Lieutenant Dan used his big policeman voice. Jacob pulled his hand away from Dan and pretended to wipe his mouth with his napkin to keep back the laughter.

The maître d' responded quickly, "I'm so sorry." He then glared at the waiter.

Chris turned a little pale at that moment and meekly said, "I'll be glad to take your order whenever you're both ready." He smiled weakly and took off with the maître d' hot on his trail.

"I think that situation is about to be fixed," Dan stated. "Now, where were we? Oh yeah, it must be my turn. I'm one of six boys. I'm the oldest. My parents are still on the farm where I grew up. Two of my brothers and their families live there, too. I've one brother who's an actor in New York, one who's a nurse practitioner in Atlanta, both of whom are gay, and one brother who's in jail for armed robbery and drug possession. Not gay. I graduated from high school and immediately went into the Marines. I earned my degrees in Criminal Justice and Law in between the three times I was off defending our country in Iraq. I live and work in the same county as you. I checked that out while you were making yourself gorgeous. I now live alone because my giant mixed-breed dog named Trina died. She lived for sixteen years and was a very loyal friend and a great police dog. I've worked my way up from a patrol officer to lieutenant, love my job, and that's about it. Your turn again." He winked and smiled at Jacob.

Jacob reached for Dan's hand and squeezed it. "I know how much you must've loved your dog. I'm sorry for your great loss." Dan smiled weakly. He could only nod acknowledgment.

Jacob stared for a minute at Dan. Silence followed. Suddenly, the silence startled him, as he realized it was his turn to talk again. Jacob folded his hands on the table and leaned in toward Dan. "Hmm, it's my turn again. I was in one long-term relationship that lasted almost five years. He turned out to be a jerk and took off." Jacob now became slightly more animated with his hands and facial expressions. "He called years later, fired, broke, and needed a place to stay. I recommended his folks, he hung up, and that was that." Jacob smiled, folded his hands onto the table, and waited for Dan to respond.

Dan said, "What a total shit! Good job. You handled that well. How about your work? Why education?" Dan queried.

Jacob's face lit up, and he broke into a broad smile. "I guess I went into education because I thought people needed help learning about the tolerance of others, but mainly because I love kids. Sometimes, I wish I still had my kids living at home."

Dan stopped him. "You have kids?"

"Yes, and it's a story for another time. Anyway, I moved to the current position I have because I worked hard and did my job. I'm in administration now and go to all the meetings like the one I'm attending here, and I bring back important information to share and reteach the things I learned to our staff. Dan, how about you? Why are you here exactly?"

Hesitating at first, Dan responded, "I'm here for a law enforcement conference and to accept an award and give a speech. I'll be running for sheriff in the fall when our current sheriff retires to be a stay-at-home mom. I wasn't going to come here and accept the award, but the entire force thinks I need to be out more in the public eye. I know that it's important to get out and meet and greet more people and let the public know who I am, so I'm here." Dan's facial expression changed from smiling to a look of discomfort. He said, "I'm not great with social situations that make me stand out."

Jacob reached across the table and placed his hand on Dan's. "No need to be embarrassed. I can fully understand how you feel. You're getting an award? For what, may I ask?"

Dan cleared his throat and met Jacob's gaze. "Last year, there was a standoff at the bank. A man held a pregnant woman hostage. I took a bullet but still managed to somehow take the bastard out. The award's for going above and beyond the call of duty. But, Forrest, I was just doing my job." Dan answered so quickly and calmly that it didn't initially register with Jacob what he meant.

Taking a minute to process what Dan had told him, Jacob's face suddenly showed recognition. "Wait! You got shot! Oh, my God! Are you okay? Hold on. I remember this whole thing. You nearly died. My God, Dan, you're a hero!"

Smiling at Jacob, Dan said, "Forrest, I was doing my job. Sometimes people get hurt in my line of work. Sometimes, they even lose their lives."

"Dan." There was much emotion in Jacob's voice. "Are you okay?"

Reaching across the table and taking Jacob's hand, Dan softly said, "Little Jacob, I'm just fine. I'm back at ninety-nine percent. You're never a hundred percent again after being shot. When I think that I served three tours of duty in the Middle East and came back without so much as a scratch, then some drug-crazed asshole comes close to taking me out right here in the good old US of A . . . it all baffles me how that can happen."

Both men stared at each other. The electricity between them was powerful and drew them to each other. It was Dan who finally broke the moment. "You ready to pick a starter? I'm starving. I'll flag Tinkerbelle when you've chosen." Dan's humor lightened the atmosphere.

Dan looked directly at Jacob. "Jacob, you know if this was

another place and time, I could get very attached to you, little guy. You're just about everything I've always fantasized about. You're smart, career driven, cute as hell, and so easy to be with. Plus, you think I'm hot."

Jacob blushed beet red but smiled, and then his words just tumbled out, "I've been thinking the same thing."

They both ordered mussels and requested refills on their drinks. The starters arrived. Dan smiled at Jacob and said, "Jacob, I've got to tell you, these bourbons are starting to go to my head a little. Glad we got some food."

Their waiter, now known to them as Little Miss Snip and Snap, had much better manners that time. Leaning into Jacob, Dan stage whispered, "I guess he got his ass chewed, since his manners have improved."

The two of them discussed entrees while they were enjoying their appetizers. Dan flagged the waiter again. Little Miss Snip and Snap took their orders without comment.

Dan ordered the T-bone with a baked potato with all the fixings and a salad.

Jacob ordered the Mandarin duck with Chinese vegetables and a salad.

"Ick." Almost childlike, Dan made a yuck face.

Catching Dan's weird expression of disdain, Jacob chuckled and then spoke like he was talking to a child. "Lieutenant Dan, you need to learn to grow beyond your small little redneck world. I can eat steak at home, and I do make a mean grilled steak, if I say so myself. However, I'd never cook duck, so I'm trying it now. Grow and experience. That's what life's about. After all, life is like a box of chocolates."

Dan was amused at Jacob's Forrest imitation. When Jacob smirked for a second, Dan hummed like he was rethinking his decision about steak, but placing his hands on the table, he leaned forward. "But it's duck, yuck! I'm pretty sure I'll never be able to eat Donald."

Jacob chuckled and then rolled his eyes. "It's like listening to an eight-year-old. So, Dan, tell me about your personal life?" Jacob asked as the salad arrived. "You know all about mine."

Dan replied to Jacob, "I know all about it? Is that it? One romance and break up, really? You're not kidding, are you?"

Jacob shook his head. "Oh, I've dated and stuff, but so far, there hasn't been that spark."

"Okay, I guess I was a little more active than you in that area. My first big romance happened in high school. Maury Charter dumped me to marry Mollie Perker because he knocked her up while he was fu—dating me. I beat the shit out of him for both Mollie and me. FYI, they're still married and have four kids now. My second romance lasted for three years, but Nick was killed in a robbery at his store while I was in Iraq. I couldn't even come home for his funeral. *Don't Ask, Don't Tell* didn't cover that."

"How incredibly sad." Jacob leaned forward and gently touched Dan's hand.

"Don't be too sad, Forrest. He'd a half dozen men or more throwing themselves on his casket. That's when a huge brawl broke out, and the police had to come after they turned over the casket. It turned out that being faithful wasn't in his character." Dan laughed out loud, making Jacob laugh, too. "The last guy was just fun and moved on. He and I are still friends. But now I want and need something more. Something I've always dreamed of, a more serious and permanent relationship. So there, you have my whole life history." Their food arrived, and it smelled and looked delicious. Dan said, "That duck does look delicious, but still, it's duck!" Dan quacked as Jacob took his first bite, earning him a kick under that table. "Ow! That hurt! It's going to leave a mark." Dan whined.

"It'll be something to remember me by," Jacob quipped back.

For the rest of the dinner, they had a leisurely meal. Jacob even got Dan to try the duck. The surprised look on Dan's face revealed that he actually liked it, although he never admitted to it. Dan just shrugged his shoulders and sort of nodded his head.

At first, Jacob was expecting a comment, but when he realized it wasn't coming, he said, "You're one stubborn man, Lieutenant Dan. I can plainly see you can never admit when you're wrong."

With a mischievous grin, Dan said, "And . . ."

"I give up."

While enjoying their meal, the two of them chatted about life and work and soon discovered how similarly they each viewed the world. Jacob leaned forward and said to Dan, "I marvel over how much things have changed over the years, how gay people can now get married and even adopt without all the red tape. They can even have both partners on their child's birth certificate."

"It took time, Jacob, but we finally got there. Although, I worry that it could be swept away at any moment."

Dan changed the subject when he started regaling the tales of his childhood antics. Throughout the evening, Jacob was thoroughly entertained by Dan's nostalgia. Jacob's hilarious stories about some students he'd taught tickled Dan.

"Dan, it's incredible how in tune we are with each other. It could be the alcohol talking, but I feel like I've known you all my life."

Dan's expression softened, and his wonderful personality came to life, "There's more to it than just alcohol. I feel it in my soul."

They were focused only on each other. They both reached out and locked their fingers together. Tenderness flowed from both of them as they looked dreamily at each other.

The moment ended when their waiter broke the magic. He

put both hands on the table and leaned in so no one else could hear him. "Do you two want anything else?" His shitty attitude had returned.

Jacob's expression changed. Jacob was not happy.

Dan said out loud, "Huh, oh."

However, instantly Jacob pulled it together and came across as collected and calm. Jacob used his index finger to indicate for the waiter to come closer, where he grabbed the waiter by his tie, yanked him in close, and whispered, "I've had all I'm going to take from you. You've been rude and disrespectful to both my policeman husband and me. I'm now going to turn him loose, and I hope you'll survive the barrage of tickets, traffic stops, and arrests for minor offenses you're about to encounter. Do you read me loud and clear?"

The stupid waiter quickly nodded and took off as soon as Jacob let go. Jacob looked at Dan. "Oh my God, I'm so sorry, but that stupid thing got to me with his absolutely rude behavior, and for no good reason."

"I couldn't have put it better myself . . . husband." Then laughter came rolling out of Dan.

The maître d' appeared and was very apologetic. "I'm so sorry for our staff member's rude and—"

"Obnoxious?" Dan filled in the blank for him.

The maître d' nodded. "Yes, obnoxious behavior. Your dessert is on us tonight. Please don't believe your waiter's behavior reflects our policies in this restaurant." The maître d' stopped and he studied Dan for a moment. "You're Lieutenant Daniel Winters, the guy that saved the pregnant girl, aren't you? Gosh, I'm so sorry that he gave you two a difficult time. We do train our staff about courtesy and professional customer service. I'll have him terminated immediately."

Jacob raised his hand and shook his head no. "That would be over the top. Instead, he needs to be retrained at the corporate headquarters and then moved to a less lucrative location.

That should teach him something about his bad behavior and its consequences. Oh, yeah, and remind him if he quits, there will be no references."

Dan sat there as if in disbelief and shocked at what Jacob had just presented. The maître d' scurried off and Dan continued to stare at Jacob.

"What? Like I want to pay for his unemployment!" Jacob said.

"You never stop teaching, do you?"

"Nope, I guess I'm genetically predisposed."

They finished their dessert, and Dan paid the check. They gathered their things and left the restaurant.

When they got outside, Dan took Jacob's hand and turned Jacob gently toward him, saying, "I'm feeling a bit keyed up. How about we go for a stroll around downtown Athens?"

Jacob nodded in agreement, and off they went.

Strolling past the Classic Center, they both spoke simultaneously, "All my meetings are here." The two paused for a second, laughed, and moved on.

Dan chided, "One never knows, does one?"

"Dan, I love your wonderful sense of humor, and you're fun to be around. I watched as your laughter came so easy for you, and it was so rich and encompassing. People seemed to join in, both at the restaurant and at the hotel."

"Thanks, Forrest. I take that as a wonderful compliment."

Crossing the street, they walked down one of the narrow streets in the downtown area. So many bars, clubs, and small restaurants crowded into such a relatively small area. Some places looked packed with younger people, and after a quick glance inside, they shook their heads. "Too young," they both said and laughed, as once again they were thinking the same thing. Moving on, they needed a better fit for them.

As they walked past one very noisy and crowded bar, three uniformed police officers came stumbling out and right into

Dan and Jacob.

Slurring, one of them said, "Look what we have here, a couple of fruity boys."

The policeman in Dan emerged. Immediately Dan pushed Jacob behind him and whipped out his badge. Taking a firm stance, he stood tall, and his facial expression turned deadly serious. The three officers studied his identification and credentials, and then one spoke, "Sorry, Lieutenant, we were just goofing around." Then young officer added to Jacob, "Sorry, mister."

Dan threatened, "Maybe you better—"

Jacob realized that he knew one of the officers and interrupted Dan. "Phillip Michael Jones, do you recognize me? I ought to slap you until that BB size brain of yours activates again! You know better than this. I taught you better than this! And here you are in your uniform, representing this fine city, and you're acting the fool."

"Dr. Easton? Oh god, I'm so sorry, Dr. Easton. I apologize for our rude behavior. Please don't call my mama. She'll chew my ass up good." Officer Jones sounded like he was nearly begging. He and his friends became contrite, apologizing again and again.

Jacob said, "I'll have to ponder that. And I'll try to remember not to mention it when I sit with her at the board meeting next week." A quick glance and Jacob could see Dan rubbing his hand over his mouth, feigning a cough to keep from laughing. Having finished his scolding lecture, Jacob said, "Now get home."

The three officers first collided with each other. Finally, one of them got it together enough to drag the other two toward their getaway.

Jacob laughingly said, "They just acted like the Three Stooges." Both he and Dan first chuckled, and then real laughter broke through.

Dan's face and eyes softened, and he smiled at Jacob with such tenderness. "You know, for a little shit, you're something else."

Jacob smiled back at Dan and said, "I know."

They continued strolling down the street. Dan, ever so casually, took Jacob's hand again. Jacob glanced up, meeting Dan's sparkling eyes, and allowed it to happen.

As they passed a bar called the Pink Dragon, outside hung several signs about Drag Shows, Dan casually mentioned that they could stop in and check it out. Jacob made an abrupt left turn and headed inside, pulling Dan by the hand.

Walking through the entry, Dan glanced around and said, "This place is much bigger than it looks from the outside." It contained a large mixed crowd — gay, straight, transexual, lesbian, as well as a huge age spread from twenty-one to ninety-one.

Jacob squeezed Dan's hand. "This looks like a fun place."

Perusing the crowd, Jacob suddenly froze and backed up into Dan. "This isn't a good idea!" Jacob said, shouting over the noise.

"Why the hell not?" Dan shouted back.

Still having to shout to be heard, Jacob said, "My ex is here and looks drunk, and he's a real S-O-B when he's drunk." The music stopped right before Jacob shouted the work drunk. People around them stopped for a second and stared at them. Following the direction where Jacob was looking, Dan located a big guy who was pawing all over the people around him. Everyone the guy touched scowled and then pushed him off and away.

"That him, the one acting like a colossal jerk?" Dan asked Jacob, nodding his head toward the human octopus.

Jacob turned to Dan and pleaded, "Yes, let's get out of here, now!"

But it was too late. Jacob's ex's eyes lit up, and he began to do a massive wave at Jacob and then started bellowing, "Jakey, baby, I'm so glad to see you." He proceeded to plow through the crowd bumping into people and stumbling around as he crossed the room toward Jacob.

Jacob's stomach tightened, and he felt the blood drain from his face.

Dan's protective nature kicked in. Stepping in front of Jacob, he instantly went into his cop mode as the drunken, staggering man approached them. The man's impaired judgment got him too close to Dan. Stopping the man's forward movement and then moving him back a step, Dan said, "You, sir, are drunk and acting the fool. I suggest that you back up and move on."

Jacob's ex stepped back, and he sized Dan up and down. In his condition, he must've decided he could take out Dan, and the idiot swung his fist. Dan grabbed his fist midair, threw him to the floor, and rested his knee on his back.

The bouncer, trotting his enormous bulk over to the commotion, loudly ordered Dan, "Listen, you drunk, don't make me kick your ass. Get off Mr. Harwick, and get the hell out of here, or I'll call the cops." The bouncer's attempt to come across as tough failed.

Dan gritted his teeth, whipped out his badge, and sternly told the bouncer, "I'm a cop, dickhead, and I want you to call nine-one-one so I can have this drunken fool arrested."

The bouncer's eyes got huge as he looked at the badge. "Oh, shit, sorry officer. Ah, Lieutenant Harwick, looks like you're in deep shit here."

The owner and manager appeared and apologized for the trouble. They rushed the ex to the back offices. The music resumed, and people casually returned to their previous activities.

At first, Jacob was angry, but then he broke into a mischievous grin. "You can't help yourself, can you? You just had to go all caveman police officer, didn't you?"

Dan replied, "Yep, let's get a drink and enjoy the rest of the evening."

Jacob dreamily said, "I'd like that." Jacob took the drink. "By the way, Lieutenant Dan, thanks for running interference for me. I hate that asshole." Jacob watched as Dan's facial expression softened. Suddenly Dan drew Jacob into a gentle hug, and Jacob went with it. Tilting his head back, Jacob agreed. "Let's take our drinks and enjoy our evening."

About fifteen minutes later, two uniformed police officers approached them as they sat at the bar. "Excuse me, gentlemen, are you the ones that started the argument that caused Mr. Harwick's injuries?"

Jacob's mouth dropped open, surprised by the officers.

Dan, on the other hand, immediately flared into pissed-off. "You got to be fucking kidding me!" He immediately reached into his jacket pocket for his badge and credentials, a movement that put the officers on the defensive, and both stepped back and placed their hands on their revolvers. "Officers, stand down! It's my ID!" Dan ordered. They instantly stood down. Pulling his badge, he flashed it at the officers. They examined Dan, his badge, and eyed Dan again.

"I'm so sorry, Lieutenant Winters, the gentleman in the back told us that you and the gentleman with you accosted him," the officer said as he indicated Jacob.

"If you look at the security video, it'll be apparent what really happened. So, you know I'll have to inform your superiors that you didn't follow appropriate protocol when you approached me and accused me of a crime." Turning to Jacob, Dan snapped, "Who in the hell is this Harwick anyway? Why are all these people jumping through hoops for him?"

Quietly Jacob explained, "Daniel, he's president of the school board in this school system and sells real estate. From everything I heard about him, he gets his strength from bullying people and getting them fired. After all, he's a fine, upstanding, married, Christian man who happens to be hanging out in a gay bar."

"Now that, in itself, could be an interesting story." Dan winked at Jacob. He read the name of officers off their badges. "So, Officer Mikkels and Officer Hooper, are there any other questions I could answer for you?"

"Are you *the* Lieutenant Daniel Winters that's running for sheriff in the neighboring county?" Officer Mikkels meekly asked.

"That would be me," Dan responded.

"I'm sorry we bothered you, Lieutenant. I assume you'll be pressing charges on Mr. Harwick," the young officer stated.

"That would be correct, and tell Reb, your boss, that I'll see him tomorrow at the meeting and want to have a little chat with him. You two are dismissed."

The officers apologized again and quickly left.

Jacob elbowed him. "Show off."

"Come on, dance with me." Jacob hesitated but nodded, and Dan led him to the dance floor. Smiling his heart-melting smile, he wrapped his arm around Jacob's waist. As if magic happened, the music changed from fast-paced to a slow-moving, romantic rhythm. Jacob was nervous, but with Dan's confident air and how he took the lead, Jacob relaxed.

Moving with the grace of ballet dancers, Dan and Jacob flowed across the floor, dancing as if they'd been doing this for years. People stopped dancing and stood staring in amazement. Dan twirled them around the dance floor. Jacob, fixing his focus on Dan and the sparkle that shone in his eyes, was *almost* unaware that nearly everyone around them had stopped dancing and stood watching the two of them as they danced like Fred and Ginger across the entire dance area.

When the music stopped, their audience burst into thunderous applause and cheered. Both men were startled at first.

Jacob turned crimson red, but Dan smiled, waved, and took a bow. A gentle nudge from Dan, and Jacob joined him in one final bow. Then off they floated into the crowd and right out the door. "Holy shit, Jacob, you're the best dancer!"

Jacob popped him on the chest and retorted, "No, you big oaf, I can follow. You're the dancer! How many lessons have you had, Fred Astaire?" Jacob smiled and asked Dan.

"Oh, that. Mom was a professional dancer on Broadway before she met my dad. Poor old dad has two lefties, so she taught us all to dance so she would have partners or at least one partner to dance with," Dan said, laughing.

Hooking his arm with Dan's, Jacob joked, "Well, Fred, Ginger's getting tired, and I've got a long day tomorrow. We better head back to the hotel."

Lieutenant Dan nodded and squeezed Jacob's arm, and off they went.

Becoming almost silly while walking back to the room, Dan regaled stories of his childhood and some of the goofy things he and his brothers had done.

Jacob had to stop and hold his side because he laughed so hard. "Was your family really that full of constant antics?"

"Oh my God, my brothers and I gave my folks gray hair for sure." Dan laughed at himself. "So how about your family, Mr. Education? Any antics you care to share?"

Jacob stopped laughing, and a serious mood came over him as he answered Dan. "None. Appearances meant everything to my family. Like I told you, I came out to my family when I turned twenty, and they disowned me. I had one hour to pack just what I could carry, and my parents ordered me out of the house. I haven't heard much from my parents, and any communications have been through lawyers."

Pulling Jacob into him with a hug, Dan held him.

Looking up at Dan, Jacob continued, "I still had the last

28

laugh. My grandfather died a couple of years after that, and unbeknownst to me, the old codger left me everything — the business, the family house, and all the assets Grandfather had acquired over the years. We were always very close, and he was the only family member I stayed in regular contact with then. He stated in his will that he disliked the rest of the family. I did love that man, and I miss him so much even to this day. But I never expected that. Now, so you know just how shitty my parents were and are, it took my grandfather's lawyer several months before he located me. He'd been given several false leads, by guess who? During that time, my parents and sisters made a desperate attempt to revoke my grandfather's will, but, much to their chagrin, it wasn't possible. I visited my grandfather the day he died, although I doubt he was even aware I was there. But at least I got to see him one more time and tell him I loved him. I was there when Grandfather died, not the others, just me. I quietly attended his funeral sitting in the back, so I went unnoticed. I really had no idea that he'd left me everything." Jacob became very sad and looked up at Dan. "So that's my life.

Dan held open his arms, and Jacob leaned into them. Dan playfully tickled Jacob's ribs. Lightening the conversation, Dan joked, "God. Forrest, are you a wealthy man or what?"

Jacob laughed. "Yep."

Noticing that they'd reached their hotel surprised Jacob. "Gosh, we're already back at the hotel, and I've managed to tell most of my life's history to an almost stranger."

They entered the hotel and remained silent until they got back to their room. Sitting on the sofa, Dan patted it for Jacob to join him. "So you're like a gazillionaire and have a ginormous multi-faceted business and a huge mansion that you could live in, but you live out in the sticks and are an education administrator? I bet you live on your current salary, too."

"Well, it's true that I do just that. I put nearly everything my grandfather left me into a non-profit charity that helps gay people of all ages. My grandfather's house is on the federal landmark registry, so it must be left untouched. However, it's a good shelter for those who need just a leg up. Anyone that qualifies can stay there for up to six months, but no longer than that. I have personnel there to help get the people trained, educated, or placed in a good job. You may know about the John Easton Sr. Foundation. It's what Grandfather would have wanted, since he was a huge philanthropist in his day. Now it's all run by my two sons my nephews and a niece. All of whom I trust to continue to fulfill my grandfather's dreams long after I'm gone."

Dan looked perplexed. "Whoa, wait, you mentioned children earlier, and I guess I skimmed past it. You told me you were never married."

Jacob laughed at his confusion. "Oh yeah, I had to have an heir, as it was a condition in Grandfather's will. Well, I had a shit pile of money and hired a surrogate, and I got my son, JJ, aka John Jacob Easton IV. And Michael was adopted when he was ten. Dan, remember, this was all nearly thirty years ago. My niece, Jovena Easton, is my oldest sister's only child and is nothing like her parents or grandparents. She's smart, sensitive, and gay, as are my two brilliant nephews, Jason Pruitt and Kato Massingil. They're from my second oldest and youngest sisters, and again, they're very normal people. The five of them will inherit the estate when I die. There's my life in a nutshell."

"Damn, Forrest, you've had a tough and complicated life. And you have kids? Holy shit, you're full of surprises!"

Jacob gently squeezed Dan's forearm. "Everything but my kids is history."

Dan's expression turned very serious, and he asked, "Where are your parents and sisters now?"

"My parents are in their nineties and live in a posh assisted living retirement facility, as do my two older sisters. The rest I don't know about or even care about, and I know about my parents and sisters because my niece fills me in about them. As far as I'm concerned, they're all on their own."

Tearing up, Dan said, "Jacob, I'm so sorry about your family. I can only imagine the pain they caused you. But now tell me about these kids of yours."

Jacob's smile broadened. "Hmmm, what should I say? They're brilliant, good-looking, loving, and caring boys, I should say men. JJ looks an awful lot like me but built more like you. Michael is small like me and beautiful. JJ found Michael when they were seven. He lived on the streets here in Athens and had been doing that for a couple of years. It's hard to believe that still happens. A five-year-old falls through the cracks and then has to fend for himself. Anyway, JJ snuck him into the car and up into his room, where the two of them kept Michael's existence a secret for almost a week. Until one night, I heard the sound of a child crying. I found him in JJ's closet. At first, the Division of Family and Children's Services tried to get involved, but my attorney shot them down. After the adoption, the Easton Lawyers sued the Division of Family and Children's Services on Michael's behalf, and they won. We didn't want a cash settlement but rather an overhaul of the system for better checks and balances so this wouldn't happen to another child in the Athens area or the entire state, for that matter. So the Michael J. Easton Law was put into effect. No more six years in DFACS custody. They've eighteen months for permanent placement, and the rest you know because you're an officer of the law. So now you know nearly everything there is about me."

Dan slid the back of his hand lovingly across Jacob's cheek. "You're my hero, little man," Dan whispered.

Playfully pushing him away, Jacob cleared his throat and

said, "You promised to be on your best police officer's behavior."

"God, I'm a terrible liar," Dan replied and laughed.

But it was getting very late, and Dan mentioned the time. They both needed to attend long meetings the next day.

"Dan, I'm exhausted. I need to go to sleep."

"Me, too," was all Dan replied. Separating, they each got ready for bed. Jacob slipped into the bathroom to change, wash up, and brush his teeth.

Stripping down to his boxers, Dan sat on the bed, waiting to get his turn in the bathroom. When Jacob came out of the bathroom in a white t-shirt and red plaid sleeping pants, Dan burst into laughter. "You look like my grandfather dressed like that."

Jacob immediately flipped him off. "Mind your own business." He then hopped under the covers on the right side of the bed.

Raising a concerned eyebrow, Dan said, "Wrong side there, squirt, unless you want me all over you all night long."

Jacob sat up. "You got to be kidding."

"Not kidding," Dan said without a hint of humor.

"Fine then, you big ox, I'll take the left side," Jacob grumbled as he slid over.

Dan took his turn in the bathroom. He sniffed his armpits to be sure he didn't have B.O. Nope, he was okay there. He brushed his teeth and washed his face and hands. "Here goes nothing," he mumbled and headed off to get in bed with Jacob. Dan froze for a second because Jacob was facing him, pretending to sleep. Glimpsing Jacob's fluttering eyelids and the tiny sparkle of reflected light peeked through them, Dan knew that Jacob was trying to watch him secretly. So Dan stretched and flexed and adjusted his package. As he climbed into bed, Jacob slowly turned away from him. Almost instantly, the blankets and spread made Dan overheated. So he just threw everything off but the top sheet.

Sitting straight up, Jacob gave Dan an I-am-going-to-kill-you look. He then started squealing in protest, "I'm cold-natured and like covers, put the covers back where they were."

Dan sat up and stared at Jacob in shock. "What? This room is like an oven, and all those blankets were roasting me alive."

Narrowing his eye almost to the point of squinting, Jacob whined, "But I'm not roasting, and I don't have your enormous caveman bulk, so put back the covers, now! Please."

Instead, Dan wrapped his arms around Jacob and pulled him in close. "There, now you've got my enormous caveman bulk to keep warm."

Within moments, Jacob heard Dan's breathing deepen, and he started to snore softly. He was asleep. Being tired from the long day and too tired to argue anymore, Jacob nestled in and soon fell asleep.

Jacob woke to a real surprise. The hulk of a man who engulfed him was still holding onto him. It took a couple of seconds before he realized how he got into this situation. Plus, there was an enormous erection pushing up against his behind. Every nerve in his body came alive.

Seeing the time, Jacob needed to stop this before things went south, or they would be late. Jacob tried to slip out of Dan's embrace, but that only made Dan pull him closer. Again, Jacob glimpsed the clock, and the realization hit him that they'd both be late for important meetings if they didn't hurry.

"Lieutenant Daniel Winters!" Jacob shouted. Dan shot straight out of bed and stood shaking his head, his manhood jutting straight out.

"Jesus Christ, Jacob, you nearly put me into cardiac arrest!" Dan shouted. Dan glanced down at his *gun* and seemed to realize it was aimed right at Jacob.

Jacob teased, "That monster looks loaded."

Quickly covering himself and turning bright red, Dan rushed to the bathroom. Lying there in bed, Jacob realized that being wrapped in Dan's arms, he'd slept extremely well for the first time in a long time. He felt safe.

Bursting out of the bathroom with steam flowing behind him, Dan was wrapped in a towel and was still dripping wet. Jacob rolled onto his side and propped himself up to get the best view.

Lieutenant Dan froze for a second, and Jacob watched his every movement. Dan scolded, "Not one fucking word!" He pointed his index finger in the air to reinforce his point, but his attempt to regain control of the entire situation failed, and he must have known it. He grumbled and huffed around the room as he gathered his clothes. Jacob started laughing, and every time Dan barked at him to stop, it made it worse. Finally, Dan joined Jacob. Dan sat on the bed and watched as Jacob rolled back and forth on the bed in peals of laughter. As everything subsided, Dan focused on Jacob. Both men could see and feel the passion between them, and their bodies started to react. For a moment, everything stood still and was silent.

Jacob broke the spell when he shifted and scooted to the edge of the bed. "Shit, I'm going to be late. I need to shower and hurry over to Classic Center. I'm leading this morning's meeting!" Jacob darted off into the bathroom.

When Jacob stepped out of the bathroom, he immediately noticed Dan. Seeing this beautiful man dressed out in his uniform stunned Jacob, but before he could gather his thoughts, he blurted out, "Holy moly! You're smoking hot!" Slapping his hand over his mouth, Jacob stood there blushing but still

34

unable to take his eyes off of Dan.

With a smile that lit up the room, Dan answered, "Smoking hot, am I?"

Jacob kept his mouth covered and just nodded.

Dan posed in the mirror and flexed his biceps. "Guess you're right. I am."

Rolling his eyes, Jacob huffed out, "And you're conceited. Today's your award ceremony, isn't it?"

Dan nodded. "First, I have a meeting with the sheriffs from around here, and then the ceremony will start around ten or so. It should wrap up around noon."

They simultaneously looked at their watches. "*Shit!* We're going to be late!" they both exclaimed. The two finished dressing and hustled to the elevator and out the hotel doors.

Jacob shouted, "Later!"

Dan called back, "Meet me at Luke's for lunch!" and ran off to get to his functions on time.

Dan had a meeting with the sheriffs from the surrounding counties first thing. They talked about crime statistics and continuing police training. Dan looked at his watch and realized they had been meeting for two hours. "Guys and Gals, I've a ceremony to attend, so I've got to go."

Sheriff Reb Parker spoke, "We all have to attend that ceremony. Congratulations, Dan. You make us proud." They all shook hands and took off for the auditorium.

Walking into the vast auditorium, Dan joined the state officials already there. Dan glanced into the audience, and much to his absolute surprise, saw his family in the front row. His mother and father came dressed as if they'd arrived in town on a buckboard. Just plain country folk, they lived by the rule that if it was good for church, it was good to go anywhere. The clothes they wore were not torn or tattered but just outdated. His brothers and their spouses were sharply dressed. Dan walked up to his family. "Mom and Dad, how did you find out about this? And what, you couldn't spring for some new clothes?"

His mother said, "I look elegant, and your dad is the most handsome man here!"

Dan and his brothers simultaneously burst into laughter.

"Mom, you've had that dress for twenty years. When this is over, we're going shopping."

The master of ceremonies cleared his throat into the microphone, which caught Dan's attention, and he hurried to join him on the stage. The ceremony took another couple hours, with the speeches and praises for Dan. He accepted his award for heroism and gave a heartfelt speech about his family and the fact that he grew up with the strength and self-pride his parents instilled in him. His mom cried, his dad pretended not to, and even his brothers looked a bit choked up. The auditorium thundered with applause. Stepping away from the podium, Dan glimpsed someone familiar way in the back that captured his attention. There stood Jacob. Dan's eyes filled with tears. He nodded acknowledgment to Jacob. He nodded back.

Right after the ceremony ended, Dan hurried off the stage, but he first asked his parents to wait for just a few minutes. He took off in Jacob's direction, catching him just as he left the Center. "Jacob, wait up for a second. Come meet my family."

Jacob stopped in his tracks and turned to Dan. His shocked expression spoke volumes.

"Please come," Dan begged, pulling Jacob in that direction.

"I am not! How in the hell will you explain me to them? Did that even cross your mind? And us sharing a room! Holy shit! They'll think I'm the town slut." Jacob didn't mean to be quite that loud, and people around started to focus on their conversation. Jacob watched as he realized people had stopped because they were intrigued by their conversation, and some around them even leaned in to hear more. Before Dan could speak, Jacob said loud enough for all the busy-bodies to hear. "What? You don't have enough business of your own, you have to mind ours, too? Move on." The crowd quickly dispersed.

Dan whispered in his ear, "We live in the same county. They'll not know how long we've known each other, and we'll leave the room-sharing part totally off the page."

Jacob shook his head no.

Dan didn't give up. "Please, Jacob, I'm feeling such wonderful things about you, and I think you're feeling them, too. Plus, you're the first man I ever wanted to have my parents meet."

Jacob whispered, "Why me?"

"Because you're perfect." Dan felt his cheeks redden as he answered.

Taking Jacob's hand, he led him to where his parents waited. "Mom, Dad, and you goofs, this is Dr. Jacob Easton. Jacob, this is my mom, Helena, and my dad, Tyson." He also introduced the rest of the family. Jacob shook everyone's hand in turn.

Dan's mom tilted her head, looked Jacob, and then asked him, "I believe I've been reading about you and that wonderful organization you've started. Are you Dr. Jacob Easton from the Easton Foundation?"

"Yes, ma'am, that would be me," Jacob answered.

Interrupting to redirect the conversation, Dan announced they needed to get to the restaurant before the crowd. His mother responded, "We'll be fine. Your dad and I made reservations, and we've plenty of time."

Jacob tried to let Dan off the hook by saying, "You need to spend time alone with your family. I'll meet up with you later."

But Dan's mom put the total kibosh on that as she wrapped her hand around Jacob's bicep. "Oh no, my dear Dr. Easton, you're coming with us. You're the very first man Daniel's introduced us to, and you're not getting away so easily."

Smiling charmingly, Jacob replied, "Please, it's just Jacob." Then he gave Dan that death ray stare that teachers gave when kids misbehaved. It made Dan cringe ever so slightly.

"So now, Jacob, how did you and Daniel meet, and how long has this relationship been happening? I know my son, and can tell he's quite taken with you . . ." On and on she chattered. Dan felt as grateful as Jacob looked that she chattered away so much none of her questions ever got answered.

They arrived at Luke's, a semi-formal dining establishment. Holding the door for his family, Dan smiled at his mother and Jacob. Dan's dad and finally his brothers and their spouses came behind them. His brother, TY Jr., tripped as he passed Dan. "You ass, you did that on purpose," he said to Dan and pushed him back against the door.

Helena stopped them with a simple, "No!" Her facial expression said *don't-try-me.*

The maître d led them to their table. The group stood still while Mrs. Winters seated everyone.

All stood and waited for Mrs. Winters to sit first, but before she sat, she scolded her brood. "We're in a very nice restaurant, and I'll have none of your shenanigans." Her glare moved directly to Dan. "Do you all hear me?"

"Yes, ma'am," they all said simultaneously. She sat, and they all followed suit.

Jacob leaned over to Dan. "God, you owe me for this." Dan's face flushed, nodding that he understood what Jacob meant.

Starting up a conversation, with a mischievous grin TY Jr. asked, "So, Jacob, is Danny boy any good in bed?" Before

Jacob could even answer, he heard the sound of a bone-crunching thud under the table, causing TY Jr. to slump forward.

"Are you just stupid or what?" Dan's mother asked TY Jr.

"Mom, I was teasing, trying to lighten the atmosphere. Why do I get the death glare after you already asked all those nosey questions?" Dan's shoe didn't connect next time, but he tried.

Jacob cleared his throat. "Well, if you must know about your brother's sex life, I'm here to tell you—"

"No!" The entire clan near shouted. Dan and his parents barked out laughter, and soon the whole table chuckled with them.

Dan leaned close to Jacob. "Now I owe you two." Jacob smiled at him, and Dan moaned as that smile sent electricity through his entire body.

TY Jr. broke the moment. "So before you two get totally lost in each other's eyes, where do you live, Jacob?"

Dan interrupted, "He lives in the same county as we do, about two miles south of me. Why are you asking?"

His mother interrupted her sons and looked at Jacob. "Dear, have you eaten here before?"

"Yes, ma'am, and everything is delicious so far as I know." She responded with the same sparkling eyes and beautiful smile as Dan.

Things were starting to change between Jacob and Dan, with Dan starting to become very tactile. Either his arm draped around Jacob's chair back, or he'd placed his hand on top of Jacob's hand on the table.

Jacob scanned the room and wondered if everyone was scrutinizing Dan and his every movement, but everyone seemed unaffected.

Seeing the passion in Dan's penetrating dark eyes made Jacob smile and sent shivers of excitement from his head to his groin. It looked to Jacob that Dan felt the same.

Lunch was delightful and full of playful conversation.

With lunch finished, everyone rose to leave. Dan helped Jacob with his chair. He kept his hand on the small of Jacob's back, never losing contact.

Jacob saw Dan's protectiveness come through again.

Mr. Winters shook Jacob's hand and exchanged pleasantries. Mrs. Winters first hugged him, and then she invited him to come to the farm soon for dinner.

Giving Dan her *mom* look, she said, "Did you get that, son?"

Dan just nodded and hugged her.

When TY Jr. stepped forward, he didn't offer his hand. He instead leaned into what appeared to be an attempt to kiss Jacob.

Dan stopped that in an instant and pushed TY Jr.'s forehead back. "Not going to happen, man," he asserted. TY Jr. hopped back to his former place and laughed. Jacob turned and stared in amazement at Dan and then at TY Jr. Dan just shrugged at Jacob and then snarled to TY Jr., "Mine."

Jacob rolled his eyes and put up three fingers. Instantly, Dan acknowledged Jacob with a wink. The Winters family finished their goodbyes and took off in all directions. Dan and Jacob waited as they all disappeared.

With everyone gone, Jacob turned to Dan. "What on earth has gotten into you? Mine? Really? Are you mentally ill or what? You're a giant ape and went all Tarzan! I can't believe you let them believe that we were lovers. Let me tell you."

Dan stepped forward and cut him off. He pulled Jacob in and kissed him right there on the street. "Mine," he whispered in a deep sensual tone, and Jacob melted in his arms.

Reality hit Jacob after a few glorious seconds, and his

mouth fired off like a machine gun. "I think you need to get a grip on reality, Lieutenant Daniel Winters. I don't know you that well, and for sure, you don't know me. I'm not yours. Aren't you getting way ahead of yourself? Plus, you gave me your word about being an officer and gentleman."

Dan shut him up again with another heart-melting, knee-buckling kiss. When he finished the kiss, Dan murmured in Jacob's ear, "I lied."

Jacob muttered, "Shit."

Dan smiled at him and uttered in the sexiest, life-draining voice, "Jacob, spend the rest of the day with me. Just nod your head so that I know you will."

Jacob nodded in agreement, but a second later, he remembered his promise to visit his best friend who lived out in the country. "There's nothing I'd like better than spending the rest of the day with you, but Lieutenant Dan, I promised to visit an old colleague this afternoon, and I can't get out of it." He saw Dan's smile slowly melt away and turn into a pouty face. However, Jacob's face lit up. "You could come with me! He's a great guy. I think you'd like him. Maybe you've heard of him, Preston Garrett?"

Dan's eyes got playfully huge, and then he said very dramatically. "Not *the* Preston Garrett!"

Catching Dan's sarcasm, he replied, "You've no idea who he is, do you?"

"Not the slightest idea," Dan deadpanned.

"Well, he was a teacher who became an actor. Preston's starred in many TV dramas. However, he's most famous for *Christmas Without You*, the first made-for-TV, gay-based Christmas movie."

Dan nearly exploded with excitement. "I love that movie! I bawled like a fourteen-year-old girl the first time I watched it years ago. I'm totally up for this. Let's go."

Jacob suggested that he should drive, but when they got to

his little compact car, Dan balked. "You've got to be kidding! If, and I say if, I could fold myself up to get into that tin can you call a car, I'd never be able to get out. We're taking my vehicle." Grabbing Jacob's hand, Dan led the way just a few cars down to his vehicle. Jacob stood in disbelief at the size of Dan's vehicle. It was a gigantic SUV.

"I'm pretty sure they don't allow tanks on the streets, Lieutenant Dan," Jacob said. "I'm surprised it has doors," he added sarcastically.

"Well, Little Jacob, I could pop them off if you want me to," Dan said, smiling as if he hoped Jacob really wanted that.

"Not a snowball's chance in hell." Jacob climbed in.

Off they went on their adventure. Dan's GPS showed that Preston's home was about forty minutes away. Jacob asked about every ten minutes if they needed to stop for gas.

Annoyed, Dan finally asked, "Jacob, why in the hell do you keep asking me that?"

"What does this beast get? Like, two miles to the gallon?"

"No! Smartass, it isn't that good, but I've a one-hundred-gallon fuel tank on this baby."

Jacob turned a bit pale. "So you're telling me I'm sitting on an atomic bomb?"

"Yeah, sorta." Dan deadpanned back.

"Stop and let me out," Jacob almost shouted.

"Honey, I was kidding. This big guy gets twenty-two mpg on the highway. We're fine, and the tank's only twenty-five gallons."

Dan glanced at Jacob. Seeing, and saw the goofy expression on Jacob's face, he laughed out loud, which made Jacob laugh, too.

When they arrived at Preston's home, Dan got out and helped Jacob out of the vehicle. An extremely handsome man appeared to welcome them. He really did look like a movie star with his curly black hair, muscular build, and sparkling smile.

Preston immediately went all flirty at Dan. "Oh my goodness, you brought me a present!" Squealing with delight, Preston stretched his arms out in Dan's direction.

Jacob grabbed Preston's sweater and pulled him back. "No! Mine!" Jacob said firmly.

"Oopsy, sorry, I didn't know, and you didn't tell," Preston retorted rather puckishly.

Winking at Jacob, Dan smiled that killer smile and put one finger in the air.

Jacob blushed.

"Excuse my interrupting your eye-fucking, but my name's Preston Garrett, actor extraordinaire. Who's this lovely man that my old, old friend brought with him?"

Looking annoyed with Preston, Jacob then introduced them. "This is Lieutenant Daniel Winters. Daniel, meet my oldest and sluttiest friend, Preston Ignatius Garrett."

Preston visibly cringed as Jacob enunciated his full name, then reached out his hand to Dan, who shook it. "Y'all follow me," Preston instructed.

It took a couple of seconds, but it suddenly hit Dan, who mouthed to Jacob, "Preston Ignatius Garrett, P.I.G."

Jacob nodded with a wicked smile. Following Preston into the house, Dan gave Jacob a *holy shit* look and mouthed the word pig again but held back any laughter.

Jacob murmured, "I couldn't agree more."

Preston's eyes questioned Jacob.

"Oh, Dan just was just saying that facelift you recently had is just amazing."

"Shut up!" Preston said, sounding only slightly irritated.

Dan became serious. "Enough. I didn't come out here to listen to the two of you bitch fight."

Preston was first to start laughing, and then both Jacob's and Dan's laughter blended in with his. Squeezing Jacob's arm, Preston leaned closer. "I like him."

Jacob whispered back, "So do I."

The rest of the afternoon proved delightful as Preston regaled them with his hilarious movie star stories. Stories of when he and Jacob taught together. Dan listened as Preston told about what a wonderful teacher Jacob had been and still was. "Dan, Jacob has the biggest heart and the soul of a saint."

Dan replied, "I'm finding that out more and more."

The three of them enjoyed afternoon tea. Then the time came for Dan and Jacob to leave. Dan stepped out of hugging range but offered his hand to Preston and thanked him for a pleasant afternoon.

Stage-whispering in Jacob's ear as he hugged Jacob, Preston said, "He's a keeper and just perfect for you. As soon as he asks you to marry him, say yes."

Jacob gave him a playful smack on the back. "Oh, hush up."

Dan and Jacob loaded into the SUV, waved goodbye, and headed back to Athens. "You know that Preston's a piece of work. I really liked him," Dan said.

Jacob replied, "He's a total lunatic. He needs a stop feature on that big mouth of his," Jacob said in all sincerity.

Dan snorted and then drawled, "You did great and handled yourself quite well."

"Humph," Jacob grunted but was smiling the entire time.

They drove to Athens and chatted about their day and how it all went. The two of them laughed at each other and themselves. Time flew by, and they arrived back at the hotel in no time.

"Jacob, I made a reservation for tonight at a super fancy place.

So break out your mink and diamonds," Dan said playfully.

Laughingly Jacob answered, "The highbrow stuff or the day-to-day stuff?"

Dan raised his right eyebrow. "Let's go with the day-to-day stuff. I don't want to look like the turkey that's dating the peacock."

Jacob turkey gobbled at him playfully.

They took turns in the bathroom. Showering and then brushing his teeth, Jacob wrapped a towel around himself as he exited the bathroom. "Your turn, big guy!"

Ogling Jacob, Dan ground out, "Damn, Jacob, you're killing me." In an instant, Dan moved in, pulled Jacob into his arms, and kissed him. Jacob returned the intense heat of that kiss. Dan stopped. "Got to get ready, or we'll be late." Dan set Jacob on the bed and darted into the shower.

Jacob sat there stunned, albeit thoroughly kissed.

When the shower water turned off, Jacob glanced at himself in the mirror and realized that he was sitting wrapped in a towel and still wasn't dressed. Jumping up, he quickly dressed. He'd just finished putting on his watch when Dan stepped out of the bathroom naked. The man stood there like a Greek god and finished drying off. Dan dried every inch of himself carefully and glanced over now and then at Jacob to see if he'd captured Jacob's attention. Just when Jacob reached the point where he nearly drooled, Dan smirked, grabbed his boxers, and began dressing in earnest.

Jacob completed dressing and turned to face Dan.

Dan's gaze froze on him for a second. "Holy shit, Jacob, you look like a movie star."

Jacob blurted out, "And you're a Greek god." Again, slapping his hand over his mouth, Jacob blushed. Dan's warm, seductive laugh filled the room. When he reached his arms out, Jacob automatically moved right into them. Engulfing Jacob, Dan put his finger under Jacob's chin and tilted his head so he could kiss him again. Jacob's knees weakened, but Dan held him up as Jacob kissed him back. Both men started to become sexually aroused. Dan pulled back, but Jacob needed more, and he moaned and stepped in closer.

"Jacob, babe, we'll have time for this later. I don't want to rush the first time we have sex. We'll be late for dinner, and we have reservations."

In a flurry of activity, the two men finished dressing, both looking handsome enough for a photoshoot.

"Lieutenant Dan, you're one hot cop even when you're not in uniform," Jacob admitted shyly.

Smiling at Jacob, Dan responded, "Thanks, gorgeous, right back at you. Let's scoot."

Dan took Jacob to Maurice's Fine Dining, which Dan described as *over the top, piss elegant.*

Walking into the restaurant, Dan approached the maître d', who immediately stuck his little pointy nose in the air and ignored them until Dan cleared his throat to get his attention. With an I-am-so-much-better-than-you attitude, the maître d' asked them, "How — can — I *possibly* help you?"

His put-on-airs crawled all over Jacob, and just as he opened his mouth to take matters up with him. Dan spoke, "Well, princess, Maurice is expecting us. I'm Lieutenant Daniel Winters, so straighten your tiara and go fetch him." Dan smiled his seductive, heart-melting smile. The maître d' scurried away but tripped as he passed by Jacob.

Dan raised an eyebrow and smirked. "Oh, you did not just do that, Dr. Easton."

"What? Who? Me? *No*, he's just clumsy." Blushing slightly, Jacob smiled.

Dan chuckled. "You're a feisty little shit, aren't you?"

Jacob just shrugged his shoulders.

A shorter, stout man dressed in white and wearing a chef

46

hat hurried toward them. His ruddy round face lit up as he came bustling through the restaurant.

Maurice ran to them with his hands up in the air and shouting, "*Mon cher ami, Dieu vus a envoyé comme un ange, à ma famille.*"

Jacob listened to Maurice, but when he looked at Dan, he saw the perplexed expression. Immediately, Jacob understood that Dan had no clue what Maurice had said, so he interpreted, "He said to you . . . my dear friend. God has sent you as an angel for my family."

Dan blushed. "Maurice, I was just doing my job."

Maurice turned to Jacob and replied. "*J'ai de la difficulté avec l'anglais quand je suis si ému. M'aiderez-vous? Vous vous êtes jetés devant ma fille et mon petit-fils à naître et vous avez sauvé les deux vies. Je ne serai jamais capable de te remercier. Vous êtes mon héros, notre ange.*"

Gasping ever so slightly, Jacob touched his heart.

Dan pleaded, "Jacob, what's going on?"

Jacob's eyes filled with tears. He interpreted for Dan. "Oh my, he says that he's very emotional, and English is hard for him when he's like this. He said directly to me, *I have a hard time with English when I'm so emotional. Will you help me?*" Dan nodded that he understood, so Jacob continued, "You threw yourself in front of my daughter and my unborn grandson and saved both of their lives. I'll never be able to thank you enough. You're our hero, our angel."

Dan replied, "And your daughter's mine, too." Letting out a choked sob, Dan took a deep breath.

Suddenly a noisy commotion came from the back of the restaurant. All eyes turned to see what had caused it. A breathtaking young woman with a small child on her hip rushed through the restaurant. As she approached Dan, a joyful sound exploded from her, not a word but a sound. She handed her baby to Maurice and put her arms around Dan's neck. He pulled her into an embrace.

Dan lost it. He held her tight, and through sobs, he said, "God, I'm so glad you and the little guy are all right."

She kissed his cheek, and he let her down. She wiped Dan's tears with her handkerchief and kissed his cheek again. She turned and announced, "Everyone, this is Lieutenant Daniel Winters, who took bullets so my child and I wouldn't. God sent him, and he's our hero."

The entire restaurant exploded into a standing ovation. Dan he swiped the tears away. The big man's body started to tremble as he struggled to maintain self-control. His chin dropped to his chest, and tears fell to the floor. His shoulders heaved, and his hands shook. All of the attention was leaving Dan with too much exposed raw emotion, and it showed.

"Lisette, you're my hero, as you let me do my job and then saved my life by starting first-aid and CPR. God has blessed us both." He touched Maurice's shoulder as he studied the little boy. "You must be Daniel Maurice," Dan whispered to the baby. Instantly, the baby reached out for Dan. Dan huffed out an emotional, "Oh, God." Taking the baby, he held him close and kissed his little curly-haired head.

Seeing Daniel holding that baby made Jacob smile through tears. The sights and sounds of cameras as they clicked and flashed everywhere filled the room. Dan gave the child back to his mother. Again taking Jacob's hand, he said to Maurice, "I think we're ready to be seated." Maurice led the way to their table and they were seated.

Dan released a massive sigh of relief. "Sorry, I didn't know that was going to happen. I hope you're okay."

"Daniel Winters, you're such an incredible man. This moment will forever be in my heart. Not only am I okay, but very proud to be here with you. You've made my heart swell with such pride for you."

Smiling, Dan took Jacob's hand and kissed it.

It was at that moment the Champagne arrived. The waiter

opened it, poured them both a flute, and left.

Jacob took one sip and then casually glanced at the label and blurted out, "Good gosh, I think this stuff is about eight hundred dollars a bottle!"

Having just sipped the Champagne, the price shock made Dan cough and spew out what he had in his mouth. "What!" Dan nearly shouted.

Maurice flew over to their table, and with a very thick French accent, asked, "Monsieurs, is there something wrong with the Champagne?"

"Oh, no, but Maurice, there's no way I could ever afford a bottle of this quality," Dan said sincerely.

Stepping back and looking incredibly shocked at what Dan said, Maurice, with a thick accent, quickly clarified. "Oh, my goodness, I thought you knew. This entire meal is my small thank you for the great sacrifice you made to save my family. There'll be no argument about it either," Maurice exclaimed passionately. He smiled and left.

Dan picked up Jacob's hand and kissed it. "Jacob, you're such a dear and special man. I'm so glad I met you. So you have a heads up, I may be falling quite hard for you."

Jacob didn't look shocked or upset—he simply smiled and replied. "Me, too."

The evening quieted into a lovely event, perfect atmosphere, perfect food, and perfect company.

Once the meal concluded, they both left tips and headed toward the door to leave.

Maurice met them at the door, hugged them both, and again with a very heavy French accent, he proclaimed, "You're my family. Come and visit me more often." Dan hugged him back.

With his nose up in the air, the snooty maître d' walked past them and stumbled, almost falling. Giving Jacob a quick glare, Dan said, "Will you stop."

"What? It's my fault he's clumsy?"

Dan shook his head; he held open the door for Jacob. As Jacob walked past Dan and out of the restaurant, Dan quietly said, "You can be a spiteful little shit sometimes, huh?"

Smiling a mischievous grin, Jacob glanced back at Dan and said in his *Forrest* voice, "Why, Lieutenant Dan, whatever do you mean?" Jacob darted off laughing playfully, but it only took Dan a few seconds to catch him. He then pulled him into his arms and kissed him.

It was getting late, and they headed back to their hotel. Both men were tired from the day's events. They strolled back to the hotel discussing how tomorrow's schedule would make for another busy day. Dan told Jacob he needed to attend two half-day conferences, both focused on training new officers on how to handle their emotions when dealing with perpetrators.

Jacob explained that he had a marathon conference that began at eight in the morning and lasted until four in the afternoon. It was going to be on the new rules and regulations from the State and Federal education departments. "I've got to admit I'm looking forward to this upcoming meeting," Jacob said.

Dan gave Jacob the most perplexed look and said, "Sounds incredibly boring. And you're excited about it?" He laughed and nudged Jacob into admitting it might be a bit boring.

Walking slowly into the hotel, Dan took Jacob's hand. "I had a perfect day today, Jacob, thanks to you. By the way, how many languages are you fluent in, just so that I know?" Dan smiled, indicating that he genuinely meant it.

Smiling back at Dan, Jacob said, "I've never had a better day in my life. And to answer your question, if you count English, four."

As they neared the door to their room, Dan squeezed Jacob's hand and pulled him close. Dan then bent down and kissed Jacob. The kiss was passionate, and when it ended, he simply stood, lost in in Jacob's gaze.

Dan opened the door, waiting for Jacob to step inside. Dan closed the door behind them, and they both just stood still as if neither knew what to do next.

Jacob broke the awkward silence. "Lieutenant Dan, remember your pledge to be totally professional at all times?" Jacob teased him, raising his right hand the way Dan had done when he promised.

"Babe, that went out the window the second you let me kiss you." Dan's arousal showed as eyes darkened and filled with lust. He picked Jacob up and carried him to the bed. Laying Jacob gently on the bed, Dan crawled over him and laid his body gingerly on Jacob.

Jacob moaned, wrapped his arms around Dan's neck, and pulled him into another passionate kiss.

Passions exploded as each man tried desperately to get closer and have more intimate body contact. Clothes came off, yet the two never let go of each other in their frantic embrace. They become engulfed in each other's passions.

Dan whispered to Jacob, "I'm totally safe. How about you?"

"Yes, safe," Jacob whispered back, and his tongue touched Dan's sensitive neck, making Dan shiver down his body. He moaned with desire.

Still, they chose being careful over impatience, and their passions spilled between them as their orgasms exploded between them. Holding onto each other for a long time, they continue kissing and nuzzling in the afterglow.

Jacob finally said, "Dan, let me up so I can get something to clean us up."

"Never mind." Dan smirked, stood, pulled Jacob up, and led him into the shower. They stayed there, embraced, and kissed for quite some time. The water washed over the naked bodies. Again their passion for each other took over, and both men came simultaneously. Finally sated, they let the shower came to an end. They exited and dried each other off.

Exhaustion now had truly set in, and both climbed back into bed. Dan pulled Jacob close and wrapped his body around him. In a matter of minutes, they both were asleep.

Dan woke first and checked his watch. It was six-thirty AM. It took Dan a couple of minutes to clear his groggy head. He gently shook Jacob. "If we both get up now, we'll have time for breakfast. We both have meetings this morning and have about an hour and a half to get ready and get there on time."

Jacob popped out of bed, grabbed his clothes, turned on the coffee pot, and spoke to Dan. "You, dear, sweet, giant man, you actually have to move if you're going to get ready in time!" The sound of Jacob's gentle and kind voice aroused Dan so much that he stood and pulled him into a hug.

Taking Jacob's clothes, Dan threw them on the nearby chair, picked him up, and placed him in the bathroom. Dan turned on the shower, tested it, and then put himself and Jacob in it. "This will save time," he said in his Officer Dan voice.

Their laughter quickly faded and Jacob cooed, "Only if you keep your hands busy washing and not doing anything else. We need to hurry, since you're in charge of the meeting this morning, and I'll be meeting with the state department." Jacob's words drifted away as passion filled the shower. Each man had fulfilled the needs of the other.

"Now we're going to be late." Jacob smiled and dried Dan's chest.

They hurried through their morning routines. They moved in rhythm as if this had been happening for years.

"Jacob, you must pack up all your stuff because check-out time happens long before we finish our meetings."

"I did that while you were shaving. I did both yours and mine."

Staring at Jacob for a moment, Dan smiled. "Meet me for lunch at the same place as yesterday?"

Jacob smiled. "You bet I will." Off they went with baggage in hand.

The time flew quickly, and noon came before Jacob knew it. However, the woman conducting the meeting was still answering questions. One of the other administrators asked for the fifth time, "But is it legal to expel a special needs student?"

Unable to contain himself, Jacob barked, "Marian, were you taking a nap for the last couple of hours or what? The answer to that question is *no*, not if that child's disability caused the behavior. Moreover, even if the child's disability doesn't cause that behavior, you have to offer services to that child outside of school unless there's placement in an alternative setting such as YDC. Now, are you listening?" The entire room applauded.

Smiling, the lady from the state department spoke to Jacob, "Thank you, Dr. Easton. I couldn't have put it better myself. I'll be calling you very soon. We need to chat. Now, y'all get out of here and have lunch. Be back in an hour."

Jacob got up, gathered the thirty pages of notes he'd taken during the meeting, and started out the door. Pushed for time, Jacob tried to hurry, but Marian stepped in front of him, blocking his exit. "Thanks, Jacob, for making me look stupid in front of everyone."

Jacob snapped at her, "Marian, you do this at every conference. You ask questions that have already been answered numerous times because you don't like the answers you get. It's not my fault your county is in a litigious situation—again. That would be your fault. Why you can't read and follow the rules and regs is beyond me. It's not that difficult, assuming you can read. Now, I've a lunch date, and I'm late." Stepping around her, Jacob shot out the door and hurried down the corridor to catch Dan, but his conference room was empty, so he rushed out of the Classic Center.

Dan's meeting had also run late, so they reached the restaurant at the same moment and nearly collided with each other. They both chimed in at the same time. "I'm sorry I'm late, but it wasn't my fault." Looking at each other, they both froze for an instant, and amusement spread across Dan's face, and they both burst out laughing.

"Let's talk about it inside," Dan said as he grabbed the door and opened it. They entered the restaurant, and luckily, they were seated right away. "So, Jacob, what held you up? I got held up by this stupid sheriff asking the same damn stupid questions he always does at these meetings." Dan winked at Jacob and took a swallow of water.

"Same here. That damn Marian fricken does this at every meeting that we've had together. Today I had enough, and I told her off. She's as dumb as whale shit."

Laughter burst from Dan spewing water. "Boy, that's really dumb."

"Sorry, Lieutenant Dan, I didn't mean to make you choke." Then they both laughed.

"Little Jacob, we've been down this road once or twice."

For the rest of the meal, they chatted and exchanged phone numbers. Time passed quickly, and they both needed to hurry back to their meetings but agreed to meet at their vehicles at four fifteen that afternoon.

When his meeting ended, Jacob gathered his stuff and hurried out the door. Dan was waiting outside the door, his arms open, and Jacob stepped into a hug.

Dan took some of Jacob's stuff to free up one of his hands.

They slowly made their way to their vehicles, chatting about their meetings.

The time had come for them to go home. Dan pulled Jacob into a huge, engulfing hug. "Jacob, I don't want this to end. I feel like I finally found someone I need to have in my life. Can I see you when we get home?"

Jacob let out a little sob. Dan tilted Jacob's head back, looking into his eyes, he said. "Jacob, are you all right?"

Jacob had two big tears rolling down his cheeks. "I'm just overwhelmed that you feel the same way I do. Yes, I want to see you when we get home."

Kissing Jacob with such passion and Jacob responding, Dan finally started to let go, but Jacob's lips reached for more.

"Honey, we have to get going. I'm on duty later this evening," Dan whispered, and his forehead touched Jacob's.

He then helped Jacob get into his car.

CHAPTER THREE

Jacob's workload kept him swamped the first few days he returned to work. He distributed the new rules and regulations he'd gathered from the meetings in Athens. Four groups of educators received instructions about the new rules and regs and how to implement them. People had to sign off that they received and understood the latest information. Every time his phone rang, he'd snatch it hoping it was Dan, but it was always someone wanting clarification on the new information Jacob had given them.

Jacob called Dan three times, and it went to voicemail, so Jacob left messages. He even texted him once with still no answer. By the third day, Jacob decided to quit his attempts to contact Dan. He constantly rehashed everything over and over again. He even chatted about it with his sons. "I really believed Dan cared for me. I can't believe I might have misjudged him."

"Dad, he's not worth it. He must be a total creep to do that to you."

"Oh, JJ, I have a hard time believing that in Dan. But maybe you're right."

In the middle of the fourth day back from Athens, his secretary asked him, "Dr. Easton, you came back from your conference so happy and full of energy, but now you look so sad. Honey, are you okay?"

"I'll be fine, sweet lady, I promise," Jacob told her as he stepped out of the building and got a shock. Right outside the door to the school board office were four police cars with flashing blue lights. He saw Dan walking up the sidewalk with a beautiful bouquet of multi-colored roses. Turning back inside, Jacob wanted to avoid any awkward situations.

But Dan shouted, "No, Jacob, please! You have to let me explain. Please let me."

Jacob stopped. Turning around with tears about to burst from his eyes, Jacob took a deep breath and calmly said, "Why, Lieutenant Winters, what's to explain? It's obvious that you moved on."

"No!" at least six officers shouted at the same time, startling Jacob enough to make him jump.

Jacob blurted out, "What on earth!"

Speaking softly, Dan came closer. "You see, Jacob, it's like this. The only communication I had with you was my phone. The day I got back from Athens, it disappeared. I know I could've just run over here. But number one, I wanted to be sure you still wanted me around, and number two, all hell broke loose at the station with a murder, an armed robbery, and child custody issues happening all at once. Every man on the force hunted for that damned phone. I got it back about two days later. Okay, I have to admit I was a complete asshole during that entire time snarling and barking at everyone, but it was because I wanted and needed to talk with you, to be with you." His voice faded as he stared into Jacob's tear-filled eyes. "Anyway, I digress. You hadn't called or texted me, so I was beyond bummed out. It hurt when I thought you didn't care about me the way I cared for you."

Jacob opened his mouth to speak, but Dan put his finger gently on Jacob's lips. "Let me get this story back on track. Yesterday, Officer Mike Reed, over there"—Dan pointed, and the guy waved—"told me that the phone I now had wasn't my original one. The department got me another phone just like it because one of those goons ran over my other one. It had fallen off of the roof of the car because stupid me left it there to grab other stuff and forgot it. They put all the numbers I normally called on the phone, and it worked as it should. However, they didn't know about you, but they'd forgotten the sim card in my other phone. So that's why I hadn't gotten even a message from you. It was then I realized I didn't have your information anymore." Confessing all this in one quick breath, he smiled his killer smile and handed Jacob the roses. "Jacob, I'm pretty sure I'm in love with you. Please don't walk away from this."

"Please!" the officers all shouted, making Dan chuckle.

Standing there for a second, Jacob suddenly turned away, covered his face, and burst into tears. Dropping the roses, Dan pulled him in close. "Baby, I'm so sorry. I'd never have hurt you for the world. Are we going to be okay?"

Jacob nodded and held onto Dan.

After a short while, Jacob stepped back, and Forrest came to life. "Lieutenant Dan, you dropped those beautiful roses." Dan stared for a second, and then the laughter started until it turned into that deep contagious laughter as he bent to pick up the flowers. Jacob loved the sound of Dan's laughter.

"I may be in love with you, too," Jacob quietly told Dan.

Applause and cheers burst forth from the officers in the street and from the people in Jacob's office.

Dan quietly said, "Everyone from the sheriff's department and school administration office now knows about us." Holding Jacob's face in his large hands, Dan said, "Jacob, the cat's out of the bag. You have to be my boyfriend now."

Jacob stepped into his big arms, turning from a slight blush to deep red and taking the roses from Dan.

"I could kill you," Jacob muttered, making Dan laugh out loud.

CHAPTER FOUR

Later that evening, Jacob sat at his dining table trying to catch up on the paperwork for the foundation and some other stuff for his job. He was engrossed in the work when the ringing of the doorbell startled him. Marking where he left off, Jacob got up, walked to the door, and flung it open.

Rather than engulfing Jacob in his arms to say hello like he always had, Dan looked upset. He grabbed Jacob's shoulders, bending down so they were face to face, so Dan was sure he had Jacob's full attention. "You answered the door without checking who it was! Jacob, you could have been robbed or hurt and worse! What were you thinking?"

Repeatedly Jacob tried to get a word in edgewise, but it was too late. Jacob's fifteen-pound male Siamese cat attacked with a vengeance! Dan shouted, "What the fucking hell! Get this thing off me!"

All the while, the cat was howling a blood-curdling screech, and Jacob kept shouting, "Si, down!"

Finally, Jacob just grabbed the cat and pulled him off Dan. "Si, that'll do. Good boy, calm down." He cradled him in his arms and cooed at the demon cat from hell. Si just curled into Jacob's arms and purred. "Now you know why I don't worry about answering the door. Are you badly scratched up?" Jacob asked as he kissed his cat's forehead and put him down.

Eyeing that demon animal, Dan quietly and calmly responded, "Thank God I have my raincoat on, or that damn animal would've shredded me. What the fuck is that thing?"

Smiling at Dan, Jacob casually stated, "Oh, that's just Si. He and his mate were gifts from the ambassador of Thailand. The Thai royalty raised Siamese cats for centuries to be palace guards, and Si thought you were hurting me."

Pointing his finger first at the cat and then Jacob, Dan ramped up his full officer mode. "Is that damn cat up to date with his shots? Why's he still hanging around me? Am I in danger of losing an eye with that goddamn thing hanging around?"

Jacob started chuckling, but that came to an immediate halt when he saw Dan's deadly serious expression. "Of course, he's up to date. He's just keeping a close eye on you, and you're safe if you don't make any more aggressive moves toward me." Jacob was smiling and batting his eyes as he tried to appear innocent. No longer able to hold back the laughter, Jacob let it out in a big burst. After a moment, he added, "He's a wimp compared to Meme and Amese."

"Holy shit, it gets worse?" Dan asked, sounding frustrated, then wiped his hand down his face. At that moment, in came a bulging pregnant black ball of curly fluff.

"Yip, yip, yip, yip, yip!" She twirled around in a circle in front of Dan's feet and then sat up and waved her paws for him to pick her up.

Dan laughed loudly. "What the hell, it's a living dust mop!" He reached down to pick her up while still eye-balling that beast cat the entire time. Meme went puppy-licking crazy. She was kissing Dan all over his face causing them both to laugh.

"You've won Meme's heart. The little traitor," Jacob teased.

Amese, Si's mate, strolled into the picture. First she growled, hissed, and then swatted at her mate Si, causing him to make a hasty retreat to the back of the sofa. She wrapped her colossal pregnant self around Jacob's legs and then Dan's.

"How many kittens is that poor thing going to have?" Dan asked.

"The first time, she had two. The second litter, she had four, and now the vet says eight."

"What the fuck? And the next time, sixteen?"

Jacob laughed at Dan's expression. "No more times. This is it. Si had the double snip a month ago, and this one will be next right after she weans her kittens."

Dan grumbled, "No wonder he's in such a fucking bad mood." Dan stopped for a moment. His cheeks blushed when he realized he'd just said that out loud. He gazed at Jacob and gave him his best killer smile. Laughter spilled out from both of them.

Jacob instructed Dan to put down the dog, encouraged him to pet Amese, and invited Dan into his home. Turning to Dan, he said, "What brings you out here?"

"I haven't seen you since this afternoon and wanted to so badly tonight that I caved, and I'm here. I think I may be addicted to you," Dan said sincerely.

Jacob reached up, wrapped his arms around Dan's neck, and pulled him down for a kiss. Dan gently drew Jacob into a loving bear hug.

"Have a seat, Dan, and I'll get us something to drink. Have you had dinner? What would you like to drink? I have water, wine, beer, and most of the hard stuff."

Smiling at Jacob, Dan gently caressed the little man's cheek. "I'll get something on the way home, don't fuss over me, but I'd love a double bourbon on the rocks."

Jacob scoffed. "Yeah, like I'm going to let my boyfriend go hungry. I made lasagna, and you're eating," Jacob retorted from the kitchen. Cupboards opened and closed, ice tinkled, and Jacob walked back in with Dan's bourbon and gave it to him. He hurried back to the kitchen.

"Honestly, Jacob, you don't have to fuss over me. I'll catch something later." Si growled into Dan's ear. "Jacob, that fucking cat of yours is threatening me again. I would hate to have to shoot it."

"Si, get to your room, now!" Jacob scolded, and the cat shot off the davenport and out toward the back of the house.

That tickled Dan. "I think he just resents the fact I still have a pair, and he doesn't." The sound of Jacob spewing something and then coughing got Dan's full attention. He rose and hurried to the kitchen, checking to see if Jacob was okay.

Waving his hand, indicating for him to come in, Jacob cleared his throat and calmed his cough. Jacob shook his head and smiled. Finally able to talk again, he countered with, "He had nothing compared to you even when he was intact." Dan's face turned red, and then he chuckled. "Here, Dan, take that seat and have something to eat."

Sitting down to a feast, Dan was amazed at the wonderful meal before him. Jacob joined him with a glass of wine. Dan took one bite of the lasagna, rolled his head moaning with pleasure, then sounds erupted like he was having a mouth orgasm. "Oh my God, Jacob, this lasagna's the best I've ever had. You're a fantastic cook."

"Thanks, and by the way, I'm delighted you came here tonight. I missed you, too."

His head snapped up at what Jacob said. Dan's eyes lit up as he focused on Jacob. Unable to hold back, he pushed his chair back, reached for Jacob, and pulled him into his lap. They kissed long, hard, and with great passion. When they stopped, Jacob laid his head on Dan's shoulder.

Dan pulled him away and looked into Jacob's eyes. "You know I fell in love with you the moment I first laid eye on you, my little Jacob."

Jacob threw his arms around Dan's neck and hugged him for all he was worth. "Me, too." Everything paused for a second, and then Jacob prodded, "Eat. You'll need your strength."

Dan paused for a second, then, as if lightning hit him, his face lit up because he understood what Jacob was implying. He wolfed down his food, cleared his plate, and rinsed it. Then turning to Jacob, Dan pulled him in close, swooping him into his arms. "Mine! Bedroom?"

Jacob nodded his head in that direction.

CHAPTER FIVE

Time passed quickly, and several weeks later, Daniel marched into the bedroom and bellowed, "That fucking cat had her kittens on my coat. Damn, they're ugly. They look like hideous little white mice."

Dan's words shocked Jacob awake. He stared at Dan in bewilderment. But he pulled it together after a few seconds. "I told you to hang up your coat. Your fault. FYI, all Siamese kittens are born white, blind, and deaf. The Siamese marking changes with age." Sitting up on the edge of the bed, Jacob pointed to the pile of Dan's dirty clothes. "It appears Meme had her puppies on your jeans and sweatshirt."

Railing, Dan yelled, "Your goddamn animals hate me! What's next? They shit in my boots?" Dan's eyes widened, and he mouthed, "*Oh no,*" and took off. He returned with his boots. "Thankfully, these beasts haven't thought of doing that yet."

Jacob smiled, "I love you, Lieutenant Dan."

Dan paused and looked at Jacob. A huge smile crossed his face. Growly, sexy Dan crawled back onto the bed. He would get into the office later than normal again. His fellow officers ribbed him about oversleeping again. *"Y'all are just jealous,"* Dan had retorted back.

In the following weeks, Dan helped find homes for the kittens and puppies.

Jacob's secretary complained, "It was easier to adopt my child than to get a kitten or puppy placement approved by Lieutenant Winters."

Jacob shook his head and gently laughed. "I know."

In the end, they all found perfect homes. Just as the last one left, tears formed in Dan's eyes. Jacob didn't tease him because he understood that feeling. Jacob wrapped his arm around Dan's torso and softly hugged the big-hearted giant.

Jacob was thrilled that they were now spending almost every evening together. He slept apart from Dan only when Dan worked nights. Having jobs that were in the public eye, they were often recognized throughout the community, and word of their relationship spread fast. If they went out together, most everyone stopped and chatted with them. The same happened when they dined — people would stop, and some would pull up a chair and join them. Most people were very friendly, but some were not.

One evening when Dan had taken him out to dine at a local pub, Gwendolyn Hessler, the school board's vice-chair, decided it was her Christian duty to inform the two that their relationship earned them the fires of hell. Stopping at their table, she spewed her venom. "The wrath of the Lord will be upon you, and you'll burn in hell. I'm going to make sure you both lose your jobs." She was performing in front of a crowded restaurant, but it turned out differently than she'd planned. When she finished her rant, she smiled smugly and turned around to ensure her audience heard what she proclaimed. But much to her chagrin, people booed her.

One lady moved up into Gwendolyn's space and nearly bit her head off. "Gwendolyn Hessler, I've known you for years, and now you just proved what a fat assed, pompous cow you are! You don't speak for the majority around here. Mind your own business!"

Ms. Hessler stood gaping in surprise. She must have finally realized she wasn't on friendly turf, so she fled the restaurant. The crowd cheered. Jacob and Dan thanked those around them.

Jacob conceded to Dan as they left, "Dan, I was embarrassed by that scene but proud that there was so much support from so many people."

Dan added, "I hate that it gathered so much attention, too, but I really loved how the whole thing turned on her."

"I bought my tickets to the costume ball. How about you guys?" Dan asked some of the officers at the station. Dan was excited about purchasing two tickets to the Policeman's Ball. The local law enforcement agencies sponsored it, but it was a community event. He called Jacob and began chattering on, all excited as he tried to tell Jacob all about it. However, police business had forced Dan to hang up before Jacob could respond. By the time he got to Jacob's house, he'd talked so fast about the ball and how it was the social event for the year that Jacob just stood there looking confused.

"Dan, you're chasing a dozen rabbits here. What are you asking me?"

Taking a deep breath, he calmly explained the costume ball and its importance. Everyone that was anyone would be there, and it would be the last opportunity for him to gather more support for his campaign for sheriff. He also added that all law enforcement personnel in the entire area would be there unless they worked a shift that evening.

"Great, I hope you have fun because I don't do costume parties," Jacob stated.

"Like hell I'm going without you. You're going even if I've got to take you as Adam before the apple incident! You got that?" Dan stepped right into Jacob's space, and Jacob took a step back.

"Dan, I hate that stuff. Please don't make me go," Jacob whined.

"Jacob, I'm running for sheriff, and not going would be political suicide, so you're going, too. You're my boyfriend, and I need you with me. So you've until Thursday to get your costume picked out and fitted."

Jacob relented, "Okay, but I get to pick out yours, too. Deal?"

Reluctantly Dan agreed, but after a moment of thought, he said with a meek voice, "Please, Jacob, just make a careful choice."

Dan needn't have been concerned. On Thursday, they went to the costume shop, and Dan broke into a huge smile. He was delighted with Jacob's choices. Jacob selected Sherlock Holmes and Dr. Watson for their costumes.

As they walked into the ball, people stopped them and complimented them on their choice of costumes. Always staying close to Jacob's side, Dan introduced Jacob to so many people, and Jacob, in turn, introduced Dan to everyone he knew. Between the two of them, they knew just about everyone in attendance.

The evening was going perfectly. People all around were wishing Dan good luck in the upcoming election.

Jacob mentioned that he needed to go and get something to drink, but Dan said, "Honey, I'll get you something. Just hold my place."

Jacob stood around chatting with the mayor of their town, the head county commissioner, and several police officers.

One of the city police officers, who was also running for sheriff, Joey Harper-Jones, approached Jacob.

Joey was staggering, his speech slurred, and his body swayed in all directions. He garbled out, "I understand you're quite the expert on cock sucking." He laughed loudly.

His invasion of personal space made Jacob step back.

Jacob's eyebrows knitted together, and his mood turned to anger. "I beg your pardon. What did you say?"

Loud as ever, Joey repeated himself. "I said, they tell me you're quite the expert cock sucker." He laughed again at his own supposed joke.

Jacob realized the man reeked of alcohol. The man's slurred speech gave his drunkenness away. Jacob snapped back, "Really? Tell me who they are. May I say, from my dealings with you, that you, sir, are an asshole and a drunken one to boot."

There were looks of disdain from the people around Jacob. Jacob turned away to rejoin the chat with the people near him, but before he completely turned away, Joey grabbed his arm. Several in the crowd gasped in shock. The commotion around Jacob attracted Dan's attention, and he moved quickly back toward Jacob. Dan's face turned bright red, and Jacob just caught the absolute fury in Dan's eyes.

Jacob heard the mayor say, "Shit just hit the fan."

Joey scanned everyone in front of him and then glanced over his shoulder. He took a double-take at Dan. Dan stood with anger written all over his face. "Take your fucking hands off my boyfriend now." Dan handed Jacob the drinks he'd brought for them. Jacob whispered in Dan's ear what the man had said. Dan's eyes got wider and then darker with anger. "Come with me, Joey. Let's find your wife so you can explain why you wanted to know about cock sucking." Dan grabbed him by the scruff of the neck and led him over to his wife. Joey huffed and whined like a small child that didn't want to get in trouble.

Dan's animated discussion brought on Mrs. Harper-Jones' explosion toward her husband. Dan returned to the crowd of friends.

Mayor Catlyn Culpepper was first to burst into laughter, opening it up so the entire group joined her. She said, "Well, it looks like he'll be withdrawing from the sheriff's race tomorrow morning."

Jacob, feeling sad, said, "Poor Debbie, married to a complete asshole. And she's so incredibly sweet."

"I love that big heart of yours, Jacob," Dan whispered in Jacob's ear.

The crowd started growing around Jacob and Dan. All eyes were on the two of them. Glancing around the gathering crowd, Jacob leaned toward Dan and whispered, "Dan, why are all these people gathering here suddenly?"

Without warning, Dan took his drink and the one from Jacob's hand and handed them to her Honor the Mayor. He took both of Jacob's hands and got down on one knee. "I know we haven't been together long, but never in my entire life have I ever loved someone as much as I love you, Jacob." Dan's eyes sparkled at Jacob with such love. "Dr. John Jacob Easton III, will you marry me?"

Acting like the proverbial deer caught in the headlights, Jacob just stood looking down without saying a word.

Then someone nudged him. "Dad! Answer that poor man before he has a breakdown!" Glancing over his shoulder, he saw JJ, Michael, Jovena, Jason, and Kato dressed up in costumes.

The five of them scolded him.

"Dad."

"Uncle Jacob! Pay attention and answer that poor man!"

Jacob turned to Dan and began, "Lieutenant Daniel Robert Winters" — but suddenly he couldn't stop sobbing and tears streamed down his cheeks. Finally he was able to continue. "I'd be honored to marry you, Daniel. There's nothing in this world that would make me happier."

First, there was a collective *awwww* from the crowd, and everyone applauded. Dan stood and pulled Jacob into a hug and then kissed him, and Jacob's kids hugged them both.

Weeks earlier, they had welcomed Dan to the family.

Then Jacob noticed Dan's family. Dan's mother broke from her family. Helena flew past Dan, hugged her soon-to-be son-in-law, and then hugged her son. The rest of Dan's family joined in with hugs and congratulations.

Things soon quieted down, and the crowd dispersed. That left just the family. They all chatted among themselves.

Jacob took Dan's hand and kissed it. "How long have you been planning this, and how did you get everyone here without me knowing anything about it?"

Laughing, Dan retorted, "Well, I'll tell you what, it isn't easy to get things by you with that teacher's eagle eye and the extreme sixth sense you have, but with the help of Mom, JJ, and Jovena, and the rest, we pulled it off. Thanks, everyone, for coming. It means everything to me, to us."

The servers brought champagne for all.

"To us!" Jacob offered a toast.

Dan put his arm around Jacob's waist and pulled him close. He announced, "One more little surprise, the wedding is tomorrow."

Jacob's smile disappeared, and he looked perplexed, pondering what he'd just been told. He snapped back when the realization of what Dan had said came to an understanding. Calmly but firmly, he replied, "No, I'm not getting married in clothes that look like I had to use Grandma's egg money to buy them. Two weeks, maybe, but not tomorrow."

Dan threw his head back, and that warm laughter rolled out. "Grandma's egg money, where in the hell did that come from? I was hoping for tomorrow, but if you could have witnessed the look my family and your family gave me just now, it wasn't going to happen. Two weeks then, right after the election. Is everyone okay with that? Also, Mom, get a new dress, and I mean it."

She slapped his arm. "Oh, shut up."

"Talk about coming into town on the egg money," Dan said and then howled with laughter as she huffed and puffed playfully at him.

The election results came in. Dan won in a landslide. With Jacob and both families by his side, he gave a heartfelt acceptance speech. Dan came across as strong, determined, and ready to take command. He also announced his upcoming marriage to Jacob and introduced him to the crowd. Someone from the group of supporters yelled, "Kiss him!"

Dan shook his head. "PDA from a sheriff isn't appropriate."

CHAPTER SIX

Dan knew that Jacob wanted a small quiet wedding at the little Episcopal chapel down the road. In total contrast, Dan wanted a huge blowout wedding with all the bells and whistles, as did Jacob's kids and Dan's entire family. So between all of them, Jacob was outvoted.

Jovena and Helena took over. They planned and organized the entire affair, but nothing happened without Jacob's approval.

Dan told everyone to gather at the Winters' farm on the morning before the wedding, so they could leave together. Dan caught his brothers, plus Jacob's sons and nephews, plotting a secret wedding night chivaree, the custom that disrupted the wedding night by stealing one of the newlyweds. Dan watched as his mother got wind of it and immediately squashed that idea. "I'll wear out each one of you with a hickory switch if any of you attempt something like that. Are you hoodlums listening to me?"

"Yes, ma'am," they answered in unison.

"However, it is a Winters' tradition to kidnap the bride, in this case, the groom, and keep his location a secret until the wedding." All of those men's eyes lit up and twinkled.

The idea came to a screeching halt because Dan had had enough and decided to intervene. He walked into the midst of the group and turned on his sheriff's voice. "I don't want to throw your asses in jail, including you, Mom, so no touching Jacob. Everyone hear that?"

The entire group sheepishly nodded, including Helena.

Dan continued, "Good, and if you were thinking about doing that to me, think again! Stop fooling around with nonsense, and let's get this wedding up and running. Mom, what preparations are left to do? How many people did y'all invite, and will Laurel Valley Winery's Chateau be big enough? Have you goof-offs all gotten your wedding attire?"

Jovena came storming out of the farmhouse right up to the group. "Y'all promised to help me, and what are you doing instead? You're just hanging out and chatting about stupid stuff. We should already be on our way to the vineyard."

Helena found her voice, and in one quick breath, she said, "Okay, there's going to be about a hundred guests, The Chateau's perfect, and the caterers are set. Jovena and I got that all done last week. Plus, Jovena and I found beautiful new dresses, and the tuxes were ordered and fitted. Now, how about you two grooms?"

Dan responded, "Mom, I have mine, and it fits like a glove. Jacob told me this morning that his arrived but needed more tailoring. He should be back any second."

Jovena cut in, "FYI, the florist screwed up the order for the flowers. Let me tell you that put Uncle Jacob into crazy-town. Don't tell Uncle Jacob I said it, but he did a perfect imitation of a screech owl over the phone with the florist. He may have blown out the poor thing's eardrum."

Jacob quietly entered the gathering and interrupted Jovena. "I most certainly didn't do that. However, I was quite upset, but I did get the issue resolved." All eyes focused on Jacob. "Don't look at me like I'm crazy. Pink and baby blue flowers aren't even close to what we ordered. But they promise to have the arrangements of mix-colored roses, just like the ones Daniel brought to me that day at the county board office."

"Aww, Forrest, that's just the sweetest thing. I missed you. Come here. Are you okay?" Dan asked as he reached out for his intended.

"I'm just feeling great. We all need to get ready and head for the Chateau. We have the rehearsal and dinner tonight. Do you all have your room assignments?" Jacob asked. They all nodded.

The limos appeared just a few minutes later. Everyone loaded up, and they were off.

The wedding party arrived at the Chateau half an hour later. A very long, large limo was parked in the drop-off area, which piqued Jacob's curiosity. He asked his sons and Dan for an explanation. JJ responded, "We have the entire place booked. I don't understand why there would be anyone else here. Only the families, the wedding party, and a few special guests are spending the night here."

Taking charge, Dan said, "Jacob, I got this. You just stop worrying yourself." As soon as the car stopped, Dan jumped out and headed into the main entrance of the Chateau. Everyone exited the limos and gathered their belongings. Each gave the porters their room number so they knew where everything needed to go.

Dan returned within a few minutes, pulled Jacob aside, and said, "Honey, we have a slight problem. Your parents showed up with two of your sisters for the wedding. Plus, they're kicking up a major fuss about accommodations. I wanted to ask you first what you wanted me to do before I fucking kick their asses to the curb."

Jacob was confused by what Dan had said, but after a moment, everything registered. A dark cloud of anger flared, Jacob's smile turned into a scowl, his fists clenched, and his eyes narrowed. He glanced over to his sons, nephews, and niece. They looked confused and maybe a little frightened. A furious Jacob rarely happened, and when he appeared, it made an ugly, frightening picture.

The wedding planner for the Chateau came bouncing up to the group. She took one look at Jacob and asked, "Is there a problem? You look very upset, Dr. Easton."

Slowly taking a cleansing breath, Jacob calmed himself and then spoke, "An elderly couple and their two daughters are trying to crash my and Sheriff Daniel Winters' wedding. You need to fix that situation before I cause a major scene."

"Now, Dr. Easton, I just knew you'd want your parents and siblings here, so when they called and asked about the wedding and told me they'd not received their invitations, I just had to invite them personally." She bubbled as she spoke with her sing-songy voice and a bobbling head. She stood there smiling her I'm-Miss-America smile.

Jacob lunged at her throat. Luckily for her, Dan caught him in mid-flight, and then he barked at the planner, "If you know what's good for you, you should run and run as fast as you can." Her facial expression changed from bubbly to terrified in a split second. She took off like a fox chased by hounds, her spiked heels clicking all the way.

Jacob pulled himself together and insisted, "I'm fine now. Please put me down. I need to kick some lousy parents off the premises." Dan let him go. Jacob walked to the main entrance with Dan, JJ, and Jovena on his heels.

Yanking on the doors, Jacob announced, "John Jacob Jr. and Maureen Easton, you'll gather your things and those of your daughters and get the hell out of here. Why would you even try showing up at this wedding? Besides, this Chateau's booked solid for invited wedding guests only, and you're not on the list. Have a good trip back."

The shock, horror, and drama the four of them put on display was an Academy Award-winning performance. Maureen huffed. "You don't have the authority to uninvite us. Only my son could do that."

Jacob stared like he was in a trance. Suddenly he burst into laughter.

As if on cue, JJ stepped forward. "Hello, Granny, I would have been your grandson John Jacob Easton, the Third, and you were talking to your former son. I would go before this hits the newspapers. I can see the headlines now." Reading off the headlines, as he ran his hand through the air, he continued, "Mrs. John Jacob Easton crashes son's wedding but didn't even recognize her only son. How do you think that would fly in your social circles, Granny?"

One of Jacob's sisters huffed to JJ, "Well, where are we going to stay? It's not possible for my elderly parents to make the trip back home today."

The Chateau's owner, Rex Marceline, had joined the situation by this point and stepped up. "Well, I'm sorry, but we're booked for the next three weeks. May I suggest the hotel down the road? I'm sure they would be able to accommodate you. Let me call and make the arrangements." Everyone stood and glared daggers at each other.

Rex returned a few moments later and said, "They have a suite available, which I've booked in your names."

One of the sisters bellowed, "Porter, take our baggage to the car. I've never been treated in such a fashion in my life."

Behind them came a melodic voice belonging to Jovena, "Oh, Mother, who are you kidding. You're such a bitch that you get treated like this everywhere you go. Now go before the cops arrive, and FYI, Uncle Jacob is marrying the head honcho cop."

The four crashers' expressions all turned to shock at that news. Out they quickly shuffled.

JJ wrapped his arm around Jacob's waist. "Dad, I'm so sorry. What crappy parents not to even recognize their only son." He hugged Jacob hard, and Jacob hugged him back.

Jacob turned to all those assembled. "Well, now that that

shit's over, let's get this show on the road. We got a rehearsal to do and the dinner that follows."

Dan pulled Jacob into one of his loving bear hugs. "Forrest, are you okay? I mean, really okay?"

Jacob was silent for a second and then divulged, "To tell the truth, it sorta hurt when my mother didn't recognize me. However, that feeling passed quickly." He hugged Dan hard, kissed his neck, and said, "Showtime."

Dan stood at the altar holding Jacob's hands as the rehearsal began with the minister informing all of what would happen during the ceremony. Everything went from very serious to absolutely stupid in a matter of seconds. Dan's brother, TY Jr., his best man, stood next to Dan. Dan held Jacob's hand and focused on the minister as the man explained everything. At that exact moment, both Dan and the minister froze. A deadly smell wafted its way to both men. Rev. Michaels stopped and then glared at Dan. He cleared his throat and sternly questioned, "Daniel, are you okay?"

Looking directly at the good reverend, Dan flatly stated, "That was not me." Dan turned to TY Jr. "Good God, man! Did you just shit yourself or what?"

It was about then Jacob, who still held both of Dan's hands, got the sensory information. "My word, I'm going to be sick," Jacob whined. Dan watched as Jacob started turning a light green color.

With her temper flaring, Dan's mother snatched TY Jr. by the ear. "Go potty now," she scolded, and he took off.

Dan then faced the crowd and snarled, "If anyone else needs to go, do it now!" He bit off every word as he spoke, his anger very obvious to everyone.

Jacob's color turned back to normal, and he asked Rev. Michaels to continue.

However, now that the sickness had gone away, Jacob seemed to get tickled, and it looked like he tried to keep himself under control. It wasn't working. It started with a little snort, and then he coughed to cover a burst of laughter. Laughter began to break throughout the crowd until the entire group's laughter burst.

Dan was not amused. He rubbed his forehead, then his hand slid down his face. "We should have goddamn eloped!" He caught the look the good reverend gave him. "Sorry, Reverend."

TY Jr. returned and had to do the walk of shame to the wedding party, with all eyes glaring at him. Dan grumbled at him, "Are you fucking through?" TY Jr. turned dark red and nodded his head. Dan rubbed his hand over his face again. "This is a goddamned circus."

Squeezing Dan's hands, Jacob, with his finest Forrest accent, lovingly said, "I love you, Lieutenant Dan."

Dan looked at Jacob, then smiled and winked. His entire focus returned to Jacob. "Love you, too, Forrest." The rehearsal finished without further incident.

The rehearsal dinner was lovely—Jovena and Helena had outdone themselves. Everyone toasted and blessed the couple. Lots of lively conversations ensued. People regaled others with stories of Dan's childhood escapades.

Dan's dad cleared his throat. "I'm about to change the mood of the stories from silly and stupid to endearing. So let me tell you a real story about my son. When he was fifteen, already near as big then as he is now, he was fishing down by the lake near us. Some teenagers threw a bag over the bridge into the water. Tiny cries came from the bag before it sank down under the water. He dove into the lake and rescued the bag full of half-drowned kittens, eight of them, to be exact. He swam them to shore. When he reached the shore, he found a sobbing little girl holding a mama kitty. She told Dan, *My daddy and brothers are mean to Tiger Lily and me.* She started sobbing. Daniel picked the little girl up with her mama cat, plus the bag of kittens, and brought her home to Mom and me." Dan's dad, sounding a little choked up, continued, "We became the owners of one calico mama cat and eight ugly gray-striped kittens. Plus, we sorta adopted that sweet little girl. Several years down the road, she became our daughter-in-law."

Everyone laughed.

CHAPTER SEVEN

Dan rose early. He'd already showered when Jacob woke and reached for the clock. "Six AM." Dan bent over and kissed him.

Jacob grumbled, "Daniel, what on earth are you doing up and dressed at six AM?"

"Well, sweetheart, there are some things I've got to do this morning and people I want to meet. I'll be back for lunch." He bent and kissed Jacob again. "Love you, go back to sleep."

Jacob mumbled, "Yeah, like I planned to do anything else. Love you, too."

Dan took off.

Meeting his brothers and Jacob's boys in the restaurant for breakfast was first on the agenda. TY Jr. shouted as he entered. "Hey, Dan, what do you have planned for us this morning?"

Jovena answered. "You giant apes are going nowhere because you've things to do to get this wedding venue ready for tonight."

Dan whined, "Aww, sweet girl, there's a fisherman's dream come true, trout stream here on the property, and the guys and I . . ."

"No!" Helena Winters's word was final. "Now, if you get everything done . . . and . . . if there's time, then you can go fishing." She glared at each one of her boys. "Daniel Robert, if you try and sneak off, I'll—" She picked up a baton she had brought with her and threatened them all.

Jovena raised her eyebrow and asked, "A baton? Really?

80

How will that help?"

Helena twirled it and flung it out. It spun away from her, and it made a full circle. The men all ducked, and then it came back to her, and she caught it.

"Holy moly! You got to teach me that!" Jovena bopped up and down like a little girl.

Helena smiled. "Later, my dear. Gentlemen, you have chores to do."

Dan organized the men to get it all done in a timely manner. It took them all about three hours to get everything the way that Jovena and Helena wanted. The room transformed into a beautiful fairytale ballroom.

Just as Dan and his group of helpers finished, the little wedding planner traipsed in with her four-inch stilettos, her heels tap, tap, tapping all the way into the middle of the venue. She bobbled her head, side to side, as she spoke to them. "Good morning, all you beautiful people. I presume you slept well. Oh my, this room isn't how I planned it. I'm just unable to live with it like this. This stuff has to go here and the grooms' table over there and—"

Cutting her off, Jovena said, "You so much as move a napkin, I'll take one of those stilettos you have on and drive it through your skull. Are you hearing me?"

Dan's group and Helena took one giant step away from the planner and Jovena.

However, the little planner puffed up like she held the trump card. "Well, I'll see about that. I'm going to speak with Dr. Easton right now!"

Dan snorted. "Honey, if I was you, and I sincerely mean this, I'd keep a twenty-foot lead ahead of my little guy. That way, he won't get his hand around your scrawny neck. After that debacle you caused last night, you're lucky to be alive. Take my advice. Avoiding Dr. Easton would be your wisest move and in your best interest."

The planner continued as if she didn't have any brain cells that worked together. "Ugh, and who would you be?"

Unable to control herself, Helena exploded, "You are incredibly stupid!"

Interrupting as he walked into the hall, Jacob took over. "That man's my groom, the women are my soon-to-be mother-in-law, sisters-in-law and my niece. The gentlemen are my soon-to-be brothers-in-law, my nephews, and my sons. Now that the introductions are complete, who set up this room?" Everyone's attention turned to Jacob. He moved to Jovena and Helena.

Jovena started to speak, but the planner cut her off. "I hate this setup and plan on fixing it." She was flinging her arms in all directions.

Jacob moved over to Jovena and Helena, he kissed each forehead and hugged them as he did. He waved to the other helpers and then backed into Dan, who pulled him in close and kissed Jacob's ear.

Jacob cleared his throat. "You'll do no such thing. This room is absolutely beautiful and just perfect. I was going to compliment you on the fact that you got this at least right, but it figures that my family should get the credit for that. Thank you, my wonderful family!"

Looking directly at the planner, Jacob stated, "Oh yeah, one more thing, you're fired! Now get out."

Rex Marceline stepped into the room, and he obviously had to have heard the conversation from his expression. He didn't have a happy face. "Nikki, you're the worst wedding planner I've ever had in the twenty years we've been open. Do you not have even one lick of common sense? You need to gather your stuff and go—now!"

Startled, she jumped a little and fled out of the room.

"Dr. Easton and Sheriff Winters, I'm sorry. She came highly recommended. How do I make this right?"

Jovena stepped in. "You're fine, I promise. However, we'll need security at the entrances. This wedding's an invitation-only. I've got a pretty good idea that we haven't seen the last of Granny and her trolls. I have a list of the guests, and if I can get access to your internet and a printer, I could print that list off, so we can get that info out to security pronto. They may try an early attack," Jovena said, acting like she was on a case for the FBI.

Everyone in the room laughed, and then Jacob spoke. "No, no, no, this is going to be a memorable day. People will be coming in from all over. If my parents show up, put them in the back of the room, and flat out tell them if they cause any disruption, they'll be arrested. Dan, honey, if possible, could we get a couple of your men to babysit Ma and Pa Easton if they decide to show up?"

"Aye, aye, Captain." Dan saluted and immediately started dialing his phone.

Jacob smiled at everyone. "Y'all are the best! I'm starving. Let's eat lunch, and then, Daniel, you and the boys can go fishing."

Dan's smile lit up the room.

Hooking Helena's and Jovena's arms, Jacob led the way with them to the dining area. Jacob whispered to them, "God, I hate fishing."

Jovena wrinkled her nose and nodded in agreement, and Helena affirmed his thoughts with a nod and a "*Yuck.*"

The entire entourage sat down for lunch. Helena stood and did a two-fingered whistle blast, which got everyone's immediate attention. She made her announcement. "All you Winters' boys hear me loud and clear! There'll be none of the normal Winters' shenanigans from now on. Do I make myself clear?"

There was an all-male chorus, "Yes, ma'am." So she sat down.

Jacob asked, "Shenanigans?"

Helena made her *scowling-mom* face and then proceeded to tell Jacob about some of them. "Yes, at every wedding we've had in the last twenty years, something's happened. At Jesse's wedding, they put a photo album of gay porn stars doing their thing, but the faces had been carefully cut out and re-placed with Jesse's face. I thought the minister would have a full-blown stroke with me right along with him."

The brothers all tried to contain their laughter, probably to avoid provoking their mother's ire. Jacob watched their faces as they tried staring at the floor or ceiling. They were clearly struggling. After hearing what Helena said, Jacob put on his teacher glare and whipped it onto Dan, who raised his hands in surrender. "I swear, Jacob, no shenanigans."

Helena continued with several other horror stories.

Jacob finally stopped her. "Okay, I got your point loud and clear! Daniel, if you want me to marry you, these monkey-shines won't happen, or I'll be going home alone. Do you read me?"

Dan stumbled for words. "I—I—I promise not to have an-ything to do with any antics."

Jacob glanced at Helena and side-mouthed her, "Do you have your pistol in your purse?"

Nodding, she opened her bag, retrieved it, and slipped it to him. Jacob took it and shot out a very large vase across the room. Acknowledging Rex first, Jacob said, "Add that to the bill." And then he focused on the Winters Brothers and his boys. "Be on red alert. I'll absolutely shoot anyone that even gives the slightest indication they'd like to pull a stupid stunt at my wedding. Does anyone need a further demonstration?" Jacob scanned the crowd with the loaded pistol.

The Winters Brothers and the Easton boys stood stone-still with their hands raised.

Jesse stated, "If any of you have something planned, I'm out. I don't plan on having a valuable body part blown away. Are you aware of where he hit that vase? And now, imagine where it would have hit one of us? Again, I'm totally out."

The brothers all nodded and mumbled in agreement, "No shenanigans."

Dan, who looked like he'd been struck by lightning, eventually found his voice. "Jacob! Give me that goddamn gun! I don't know how many laws you've just broken."

Jacob quickly handed it to Helena, and in a blink of an eye, she re-pursed it.

Jacob, with a sweet innocent voice, responded, "What gun?"

Dan's face turned so red that he looked about ready to explode, and his hand rubbed across his face. Finally taking a deep breath, Dan turned to the guys. "I'm going fishing." They all crowded out the door.

Someone in the crowd of men blurted out, "I nearly shit myself when he blew out that vase. Dan, you're going to have your hands full."

Dan countered jovially, "Yeah, ain't it great?"

CHAPTER EIGHT

The men returned at five that afternoon. They came barreling into the Chateau loud and noisy. All of them arrived soaking wet and filthy. Their playful laughter filled the hall.

Jovena and Helena took one look and charged toward them. However, Jacob cut the ladies off and reached the men first. He took Dan's arm. Dan's eyes bounced around the room, and he bowed his head, folding his hands down in from of him like he was about to get scolded, but Jacob only asked, "Did you and the boys have a good time?"

"The best ever!" Each man held up several trout. Rex had summoned several kitchen assistants to come and collect the fish.

Jacob smiled and reminded them, "Y'all need to hurry and get cleaned up. We have a wedding in about an hour." The horde scurried off in all directions. Only Dan remained with Jacob. Jovena and Helena stood off to the side, unnoticed.

Jacob took Dan's hand.

"You know, Forrest, you really are the best! It's why I love you." Dan bent down and kissed him.

"I love you, too, Lieutenant Dan, but you're stinky and in need of a shower. Now scoot and get ready."

Dan hurried away, smiling as he ran in the direction of the room.

Jacob noticed the ladies and waved them over. Jovena walked up and hugged her uncle. "Uncle Jacob, you're just the best! Helena and I were so mad that we were about to chew someone's arm off. In you stepped and charmed them all. You know they'll be ready in record time."

Jacob smiled and gathered the women. "I just knew they needed to blow off some steam, and now that they did just that, we'll have peace. Boy, did you smell that lot?" Jacob noted the time. "God, we need to move it. There's a wedding to be had in fifty minutes!"

Dan was amazed. Looking around, he noted the wedding ceremony venue was just beautiful. Large bouquets of multi-colored roses lined the walls and were placed all around the room. It looked like a rose garden. There were white ribbons and streamers that looked like they were all floating. It gave the room a fairytale chapel look. The room where the reception would take place had shiny satin tablecloths, large round tables, and the same roses in the center of each table.

Dozens of people arrived, and as they entered the chapel venue, they oohed and aahed at the beautiful setting. Family members helped by welcoming guests and ushering people to their seats.

Jacob was right. His parents and sisters arrived in time to make a show, but Jovena corralled them into a private room and gave them their behavior instructions. She had the backup of two burly officers. Jovena stated to the officers and just loud enough for this group, "If they misbehave at all, just shoot the old lady, and the rest will comply." Jovena and her grandmother locked into a nasty stare-down, but the old lady backed down first. Jovena's mother didn't even try. The uninvited guests went to their assigned seats and sat without further fuss.

The music started. Entering at opposite sides, Jacob and Dan met in front of Father Michaels. Stopping everything for a moment, Dan stepped closer to Jacob and then pinned his Lieutenant's bars on Jacob's lapels. "For you, Forrest."

Jacob's tears rolled down his cheeks. "You had to make me cry, didn't you?"

Father Michaels cleared his throat, and that brought the grooms' attention back to the program.

Father Michaels began, "We're gathered because those of like minds and hearts want to declare their love for each other in the bond of holy matrimony. They come to be joined as one. Should anyone have just cause to object to this union, speak now or forever hold your peace."

There were some shuffling sounds. Dan felt his eyes go wide and said, "I promise that had nothing to do with my family."

Jacob nodded and whispered, "Remember, I've got crazy family, too."

The ceremony continued. The two men repeated the vows that Father Michaels told them, and then it was time for them to exchange their own. Meeting Dan's gaze, Jacob vowed, "You taught me what love's all about. You never once doubted we'd be here doing this. I now know what love means. Thank you for becoming my husband." He placed the gold band on Dan's finger.

Smiling broadly, Dan still couldn't stop the tears from flowing down his face.

Dan took Jacob's hands, and said, "You saved me. First by giving me shelter and then by showing me what love's supposed to be like. You saved me, Jacob. Thank you for becoming my husband." Dan placed the ring on Jacob's finger and then pulled him into a kiss.

The guests applauded, and some of the officers whistled. Dan and Jacob held up their clasped hands for a second and then walked down the aisle and into the main hallway area. The two of them joined Michael, JJ, Jovena, Kato, Jason, Helena, Tyson Sr., and Dan's other brothers and their spouses in the reception line that led into the banquet hall.

So many people passed through the line—lawyers, doctors, students, teachers, police officers, firefighters, mayors, and dozens of other friends and family. For the next hour, Dan and Jacob were busily welcoming their guests. No one noticed until it was too late that Jacob's parents and sisters stood right in front of them. Dan's eyes widened and he swallowed hard.

Smiling and as charming as ever, Jacob simply said, "Thank you for coming." His parents shook his and Dan's hands and moved through the line. Jacob's sisters just nodded.

Dan nudged Jacob and said, "Great job. You're the most dignified gentleman I know. God, I love you, Jacob Easton."

"It's Easton Winters, I'll have you know." Jacob retorted.

Dan took Jacob's hand and led him to the dance floor, giving Jacob his killer smile. Dan waltzed him all over the dance floor, and as if under a spell, everyone stood still, eyes locked on them in awe. When the music ended, Dan and Jacob stopped, and TY Jr. announced, "Ladies and gentlemen, may I introduce you all to Mr. Daniel Winters and Mr. Jacob Easton Winters." The guests applauded.

The grooms moved to the table to cut the wedding cake. Dan looked up mischievously as he held the piece of cake meant for Jacob, but after one glance at the expression on Jacob's face, Dan's mischievous look disappeared.

The rest of the parties mingled and chatted or danced.

Dan and Jacob's family and friends offered endearing toasts to the new couple.

Ringing the Champagne glass with his spoon, Jacob's father stood. The room went silent. Jacob's sons, niece, and nephews move toward his parents. Jacob's father spoke, "I find this entire gathering a farce. Moreover, you'll soon learn that this old man still has a few tricks up his sleeve."

Dan followed as Jacob stood, his hand protectively on

Jacob.

JJ interrupted the elder Easton. "Mr. Easton, if you're referring to the fake last will and testament of John Jacob Easton Senior you submitted to the courts two weeks ago, I'm here to inform you that attempt failed miserably. In fact, the Easton Foundation's attorneys have found that you've committed fraud. The Honorable Judge Lester Timber agreed, and after reviewing the case, he turned the entire matter over to the DA's office. Oh yeah, one more thing, I'd get a new attorney if I were you, since yours is up for disbarment. Now, if y'all would kindly get up and leave, it would be appreciated."

Three bulking policemen helped them up and out, and this time there wasn't any huffing or puffing. They just scurried out of the hall.

Jacob moved to stand next to JJ. "Son, why didn't I know about this?"

JJ smiled and answered, "Because you aren't the CEO of the Easton Foundation. I am, and I do my job quite well, if I say so myself."

Jacob smiled and hugged his son.

JJ nodded his approval to Dan, and he then smiled at Jacob.

Dan reached for Jacob's hand and led him to the dance floor one more time. They danced like Fred and Ginger all around the entire dance floor, then encouraged everyone else to get up and dance the last dance.

It was a beautiful wedding. *Sometimes fairytales do come true.*

Life settled in right away for Dan and Jacob. Dan told everyone that they complimented each other in nearly every way. After much discussion, and with persuasion from Dan, it was decided that Jacob's house fit them better than Dan's, as Jacob had more room and acreage. However, they quickly realized that Dan needed a much larger office and a total mancave. So they hired an architect and a builder to add to the house. They both decided the modifications would make it *their* place, not just Jacob's. Together they planned, designed, and built a reasonably large addition. Even though the construction tore up the house, they held it together for the four months needed to complete the work, and both men loved the final results. A nice-sized combo office and mancave for Dan, four extra bedrooms, and three extra baths completed the desired modification. Life was good for them.

CHAPTER NINE

D r. Jacob Easton-Winters was notified to appear before the school board for a special emergency meeting.

The idea that a meeting was called without justification of any kind pissed Dan off. It made matters worse that Jacob decided to go without him. "Jacob, something doesn't smell right about this. You shouldn't be so stubborn about me coming."

"Lieutenant Dan, I'm a big boy and can handle whatever it is."

"Forrest, how often do you need to be reminded it's Sheriff Dan?" Dan chided and pulled him in for a hug.

Just two hours later, Jacob entered the boardroom, where the superintendent, assistant superintendent, entire school board, and school attorney all sat at a table. They placed a single chair out in front of them. After freezing, Jacob stared silently at the entire setup and carefully gathered his thoughts.

Jacob's brows knitted, and he frowned before he cleared his throat and said, "This looks like an inquisition, not a meeting, as you stated in the email requesting my presence. So we'll halt this now, and I'll reschedule this so-called meeting. Seeing you found it necessary to have the school attorney present, I'll need time to have legal and professional representation. Let me make this clear . . . this situation was handled improperly. It won't be in the next meeting." Jacob got out his phone and typed on it while the inquisition members sat gaping at him.

Before anyone spoke, Dan barged through the door. He scanned around the room, noticed the anguish on Jacob's face, and then barked, "What the hell is this?" Dan pointed to the table of school administration and school board members and then to the lone chair that sat in front of them.

Gwendolyn Hessler cleared her throat, and she acted as the spokesperson. "This proceeding's none of your business, Sheriff Winters."

Dan snarled at her and spoke to Jacob. "Dr. Winters, are you ready to go?"

Jacob studied his phone again and took a second to process the information. "We'll reconvene this meeting tomorrow morning at ten. Within the next hour, I'll expect a letter from you explaining in detail what this meeting entails. So you're fully informed, I'll have legal and professional representation. Good day."

The school board members all turned and looked at Gwendolyn Hessler. Stumbling through some poor excuse, she finally said, "The proof will be forthcoming soon enough."

Jacob phoned JJ as they walked down the hall to his office. He told JJ about how they had set up the room and the lone chair. When he mentioned the school's attorney, JJ agreed something was up.

He told his dad he'd get back to him and hung up.

By the time they reached Jacob's office, JJ had called back, and the attorneys would be there tomorrow, as would representatives from NEA and GAE, the two education associations in which Jacob had a membership.

Less than twenty minutes later, a school resource officer was standing outside Jacob's office door. Scowling, Dan went into sheriff mode. "Ricky! What the hell are you doing?"

"That school board member" —he consulted at his pad—

"Gwendolyn Hessler ordered me to keep everyone out, including Dr. Easton. A couple of hours ago, she went in there. I heard her shuffling things around and opening and closing drawers. She came out with an empty box, then ordered me to keep the office off limits to everyone."

Dan said angrily, "Ricky, she doesn't have the authority to have you leave your assigned post. Only I do. Also, what do you mean she was in his office?"

Ricky's voice sounded shaky. "She had me unlock his office, and then Hessler carried in a box of stuff, and it sounded like she was opening and closing drawers. After a few minutes, she carried out an empty box. She then told me to guard the door and not let anyone enter. Like I just said."

Jacob threw his door open and turned to Ricky. "Do you know what was in the box when she entered my office?"

Ricky shrugged. "Some fliers, I think. I just glimpsed the top stuff, and they were face down."

Dan stopped Jacob from entering his office. "No, honey, this is a setup. Stay out of here and let me do this the right way. Ricky, you're here under my orders that no one enters here. And I mean no one. Understood?"

Ricky nodded that he understood.

Dan took Jacob down one door to Jacob's secretary's office. "Hey, Nancy, Jacob needs to make some phone calls. Can he do it here in your office?"

Nancy spoke gently, "Dr. Easton Winters are you okay?"

Jacob started to crumble and couldn't keep his voice from shaking. "No, I'm not." Tears welled up in his eyes.

Dan pulled him into a hug. "Not here and not now, Jacob! Listen to what I'm saying."

Stepping back, Jacob shook his head and collected himself. "I'm fine," he insisted.

Dan smiled at him and then lifted Jacob's chin, looking right at him. "I'll be back within the hour."

Jacob's secretary closed her door and locked it. Jacob made several phone calls that included his lawyer and the NEA state representative. He then heard someone shouting outside the office, but rather than checking it out, he decided to wait for Dan.

True to his word, Dan returned within the hour, and he brought the city police chief, several of his deputies, two GBI agents, and the district attorney.

Right away, Dan encountered Gwendolyn Hessler, who screeched at Ricky to get out of her way. "The superintendent and I need to search Dr. Easton's office." However, Ricky stood his ground.

Acting like she was now in charge of the entire school system, Gwendolyn Hessler charged up, got into Ricky's face, and rudely said, "You're fired!"

Stepping in between Ricky and Hessler, Dan started chuckling. "Lady, you may be on the school board, but you have zero authority to hire or fire my officers."

Suddenly turning dead serious, Dan spoke directly to Hessler. "I have a court order sealing this office until the team of experts arrives to lift any fingerprints and gather all the stuff you planted in Dr. Easton-Winters' office."

Dan's attention turned to the superintendent. "Carl, your head IT guy says Ms. Hessler signed on and used a computer in the boardroom. He said much of what she viewed on the computer was child pornography. Plus, she sent dozens of things to be copied to the main printer here in the building. He's pulling that history now."

Jacob joined Dan and stood there silently, looking slowly from one person to the next.

The superintendent's eyes popped wide open, and he stared for a moment at Gwendolyn Hessler. He took a step away from her and announced, "Everyone here in the building will cooperate with the sheriff's department."

Clearing his throat, Dan spoke directly to Carl. "Well, Carl, I'm here to be sure nothing gets tampered with. The Georgia Bureau of Investigation team will do the rest."

Gwendolyn Hessler fainted.

Because of Dan's careful planning, the incident became a mess for Hessler and the school board. The GBI found dozens of pornographic pictures of young boys and men. GBI also found Gwendolyn's fingerprints all over them. They arrested her the following day as she was packing her car for what looked to be a long trip. She screamed and threatened everyone the entire time they were arresting her and while they took her fingerprints, but to no avail.

Jacob never understood what had possessed her to engage in such malicious behavior. For the following weeks, Dan stayed close to Jacob the entire time, fussed over him, and checked and rechecked with him to ensure he was doing okay.

The so-called *meeting* never happened.

Gwendolyn Hessler's prosecution followed. The judge gave her probation and banned her from ever entering any part of the school system. He also slapped her with a substantial fine. Her husband divorced her, and she left the area.

CHAPTER TEN

Spring came, and life was good for Jacob and Dan. Over breakfast one morning, Jacob told Dan, "Will I ever really get over the fact that after thirty-some years, the school board and the school administration questioned my integrity and morality?"

Dan gently patted his shoulder in support. Yet Dan knew that in spite of all his doubts, Jacob continued to do the best job possible for the system.

Several weeks later, while they were dining out, Jacob said, "Dan, I think I want to retire at the end of this school year."

Looking up from his food, Dan coughed, slightly choking on his dinner. Jacob's words surprised him, but when he got it together said, "Jacob, sweetheart, you love your job, and you're good at it. Are you sure this is a good decision?"

"Dan, I just don't feel the same about the school system anymore. Dr. Gloria Hampton, from the Georgia Department of Education, has been hounding me for years to take the state position of District Due Process Investigator for this area. Maybe I want to do that."

"Jacob, I've got your back no matter what you decide. I love you, Forrest."

"Why, Lieutenant Dan, you're nothing but a big flirt!"

Spring break started for the school system, so Jacob was off, and Dan had decided to take a week's vacation so the two of them could spend some downtime together. They planned on just staying home and relaxing because they needed it after the whirlwind of a year they'd both gone through.

They worked on the house and in the gardens. Dan took a few official phone calls but never went into the office. The two of them enjoyed Saturday, Sunday, and Monday. They spent much of their time just being together. On Tuesday morning, Dan lay in the bed with Jacob curled up in his arms, sated from lovemaking. Looking at the clock, it read eight AM. Dan whispered, "I'm never letting go of you. I love you so much." Just as Jacob started to reply, someone started ringing the doorbell, pounding on the door, ringing the bell, and banging on the door, back and forth endlessly.

"What the fucking hell!" Dan shouted and threw back the covers. Quickly pulling on some sweats and a t-shirt, Dan tumbled down the hallway. By the time he reached the door to open it, his face was red, and his movements were quick and deliberate. Feeling as though his temper was nearly ready to explode, he shouted, "Fucking stop already!"

Yanking open the door, Dan saw an older lady standing there with two tiny children.

"Watch your goddamn mouth, bud! There are two babies here, fuckhead."

He sheepishly responded, "Yes, ma'am." Shaking his head, Dan pulled himself together. "Old woman, what are you doing banging on my door at this hour?"

She snarled at Dan. "Who are you calling an old woman? You Sheriff Winters?" Dan nodded. That was when Jacob nudged up next to him.

The woman started again. "Well, that fu—"

Jacob put up his hand and said very firmly, "No more trash talk."

She nodded and continued, "Both your brother and my daughter are dead. So DFACS bringed these young uns to my house. I ain't able to keep em, and if I don't find a family member to take em in, they go into that fucked up system."

Jacob scowled at her.

"That bit—errs—I mean—cow in the car is a social worker, and she's drooling to get her hands on these here kids."

"Your brother?" Jacob asked Dan.

"Beats me." Dan shrugged.

Jacob's focus turned to the two small children. Then stepping into action, Jacob took the baby from the older woman and then stooped down to the little guy who held onto the woman's dress with one hand and his other arm wrapped around a floppy-eared doggie and his thumb in his mouth. Jacob softly said, "Hello, I'm your Uncle Jacob, and this is your Uncle Dan. Would you like to come in and get to know us?"

A very confused-looking Dan offered the boy his hand. The little guy's eyes widened, but he let go of the older woman's dress, took Dan's hand, and followed them inside the house. Jacob walked in and sat on the sofa with the baby while Dan put the toddler on the sofa and joined them.

Jacob smiled and then asked the little guy, "Is this your baby brother or baby sister?"

Pulling his thumb out of his mouth, the little boy answered, "Dat BeeBee." Then he immediately stuffed his thumb back in his mouth.

Jacob looked to the grandmother for clarification. "Her name's Belle Bijou and some other shit. It's a stupid name, but it's the one my daughter, Kerri, stuck her with. I'm guessing she's about twelve months old, maybe more, but she's tiny. The boy's two or two and a half maybe, and named after your shithead jailbird brother, Randal Junio, but they called him RJ. Okay, that's about all I know."

Dan leaned over to whisper in Jacob's ear but instead got a whiff of the baby. "Holy mother of God, when was this kid last changed or bathed?"

"That DFACS woman in the car has that stuff. She got called because that's what the cops do when someone over-doses and kids are involved," stated the grandmother. Dan rose and shot out the door in a flash. He returned in a few minutes with the DFACS lady right on his heels.

Jacob looked up just as she entered their home. He held up his hand and commanded, "Stop! You've gone far enough." The DFACS lady stopped dead in her tracks, but she bucked up and looked ready for a fight.

Glaring, she spoke quite harshly to Jacob, "I'm Delores Backner, supervisor of the DFACS in this county. I have got to inspect this house to be sure it is fit for these children to live in."

Dan turned to her and quickly responded, "What? Who said anything about them living here?"

Delores nodded toward the grandmother. "She told me that you were their uncle and would take them in. That's what brought us here. So I need to be sure I approve of this place-ment."

Jacob asked, "Do you know who we are?"

Dolores scrutinized him up and down and then scrutinized Jacob. "No, and I don't care. I have a job to do."

Jacob stood up.

Dan took one glance, then he made a goofy face and mut-tered to little RJ, "Uh oh."

The little boy giggled.

Jacob hit full teacher-administrator-protective-dad mode. "Grandmother, did you grant custody to DFACS?"

The grandmother huffed. "Hell no, I'd never do that."

Jacob continued, "Ms. Backner, you have no authority here. These children are in the care of family and in not your cus-tody, so you need to just leave."

Ms. Backner bristled up. "Who do you think you are?"

Practically growling as he stood, Dan stepped in between her and Jacob and announced, "I'm Sheriff Daniel Winters, and this is my spouse Dr. Jacob Easton-Winters. He was and is the prime motivator for the Michael Easton Law that you're not following. Ms. Backner, so you know I'll be calling the Department of Family and Children's Services in Atlanta directly. Now get out of my home."

Looking terrorized, she fled the house with the grandmother right on her heels, shouting, "You stupid bitch, you're my ride home. You best wait on me."

Jacob gathered the stuff they'd gotten from DFACS and picked up the baby. Dan took RJ by the hand and followed them into the kitchen. Jacob immediately started stripping the baby's filthy, smelly clothes off. He asked Dan to run warm water in the sink.

Dan's expression certainly indicated that he thought Jacob had lost his mind. "Why do you need warm water in the sink?"

Looking puzzled, Jacob responded, "To bathe this dirty baby."

Totally freaking out, Dan shouted, "That baby's totally shitty from head to toe, and you're going to bathe her in the sink we use for cooking and stuff? Have you lost your mind? For God's sake, use the tub in the bathroom!"

"Dan, for heaven's sake, people have bathed children in the kitchen sinks since the first kitchen sink. Besides, I'll have to drain and refill the water several times. This is the quickest and easiest way. Besides, that's why we have bleach to kill the bacteria and clean the sink afterward." Jacob calmly placed the baby in the water.

The water was instantly dirty. As the water darkened, Dan turned green. "I swear I'm going to puke. I'll never be able to use that sink again."

Laughing at Dan, Jacob chided, "Shut up, you big girl. Get

us a pen and paper." Jacob drained the water and refilled the sink again, and Daniel retrieved the paper and pen. Glancing at Dan, Jacob said, "Good, you got paper. Now write these things down . . . diapers . . . the ones for around fifteen-pound babies. Baby bottles. Baby cereal. Baby carrots, peas, pears, bananas, and baby meats . . . both chicken and turkey. Baby clothes, nine to twelve months, and that would include tees, pajamas, bibs, pants, tops, dresses, socks, and shoes. RJ, do you wear big boy underwear or pull-ups?"

RJ pulled his thumb out of his mouth with great pride proclaimed, "I a big boy, po wups. Wat wam po wups."

Looking absolutely confused, Dan asked Jacob, "Wat wam?"

"Batman, Sheriff. Boy, you're behind the times." Jacob laughed out loud, and that caused the baby and RJ to laugh, too. The precious sound of children's laughter set Dan to chuckling, too. "We'll need all the larger-sized clothes for our little man here, too, won't we, RJ?"

The little boy just nodded his head.

Dan turned to Jacob. "Honey, what are we going to do about these kids?"

Jacob finished Bee Bee's bath and dried her off. He then handed her to Dan, who went immediately on high alert. "I'm not taking that naked baby. Put some clothes on her." He turned several shades of red and backed away.

"Dan, you need to hold her because I have to find the diapers and to sort out clothes for her to wear." Jacob sounded exasperated.

"Forrest, I ain't holding that naked baby," Dan firmly stated, crossing his arms, but as soon as he caught Jacob's facial expression that clearly said, *Hold this baby or else,* he took her. But he held her out at arm's length and grumbled, "She had better not pee on me." His eyes widened. "Or anything else either!"

Laughter exploded out of Jacob. "See, BeeBee, the big bad sheriff is just a big baby, too."

BeeBee laughed. She looked up and reached for Dan, then said, "Hi."

Dan couldn't resist that precious little girl and pulled her close. She then snuggled into Dan's arms.

Jacob gathered what he could and took the baby to dress her. "Sheriff, you need to call your mom and tell her what's happening. She probably already knows about your brother and what happened to him, but I'll bet cold, hard cash she has no clue about these precious babies."

Dan dialed his parent's phone number. His mom answered after one ring.

Jacob was half listening and continued dressing the baby as Dan talked to his parents. "Hey, Mom and Dad. Yeah, I just heard. Right there in prison? Huh. I guess it's sad? I mean, it's sad. Mom . . . Mom . . . Mom! There's more. Randy was not only into drugs, but somewhere along the way, he took off time from that to produce two little ones. A two or two-and-a-half-year-old son, Randal Junior, aka RJ. Now we've got two something Juniors in our family, and a twelve-month-old girl named Belle Bijou, aka BeeBee." Dan listened for a response and then said, "Mom? Mom? Dad?" Dan stared at his phone with a shocked expression. "They fucking hung up on me."

Jacob smiled and reminded him, "Mind your filthy mouth. She hung up because she was wasting time talking to you. I'm guesstimating that she should be here in about ten minutes."

"Jacob, for f—gosh sakes, she'd have to drive eighty miles per hour to get here in that time." Dan paused for a second. "Oh, God, she would do that, wouldn't she?" Dan slapped his forehead, then rubbed his hand around his face.

Jacob had just finished bathing and dressing RJ when Helena came barging through the front door. "Where are these precious babies?" she shouted.

"In the kitchen," Dan answered.

She flew into the kitchen.

Ashen-faced Tyson Sr. followed her into the room. He took the first seat he found and sat there a minute, panting like he couldn't catch his breath. He finally squeaked out, "She damned near killed about three dozen people and us. She was a woman possessed. We took the corner to your street on two wheels."

Someone knocked at the front door. Dan left to answer it.

Jacob overheard shouting that sounded like Officer Ricky. He shouted at Dan, and Dan shouted right back. "Your mother's a menace to our entire county. She tore through town at eighty-five miles per hour. Sheriff, she nearly killed people and refused to pull over. She's under arrest."

"Ricky, I'll handle this, goddamnit. Now back off." Dan's anger spewed right back at Ricky.

The entire time Helena lay on the floor mesmerized by her newest grandchildren. She was only focusing on her two precious babies, totally deaf and blind to anything else around her. She looked up at Jacob and said, "This baby boy looks exactly like Randal, and that beautiful baby girl over there is the spitting image of me when I was her age." Tears rolled down her face.

Storming back toward the kitchen, Dan barked, "Mother!"

However, Jacob met him before he came through the door, putting his hands on Dan's chest and stopping him. "No, Daniel, not now. That'll come later. She's both grieving and celebrating. Give her some time."

Fury showed all over Dan's face until his eyes met Jacob's, and then his expression visibly softened momentarily, but flashed back when his attention snapped to his mother again.

Jacob pulled Dan's chin down so Dan was looking directly at him, then asked over his shoulder, "Helena and Tyson, will you two babysit these little guys until Dan and I get back? We need to do some kid shopping. There's some food in the bag on the table and some diapers, too."

Helena looked up at them, tears smearing her makeup. Then she glanced at her husband and spoke for them both. "You bet we'd take care of these precious little ones."

Jacob pushed Dan out of the kitchen. "Let's go. We have major shopping to do. No matter what, they're going to need some things."

Dan followed but protested. "Why are we shopping? Forrest, you're planning on keeping those little rugrats, aren't you?"

A loving smile grew across Jacob's face. "Daniel, they're family, they need us, and we're more than able to help. What more do I need to say?"

Walking out the door and toward his car, Dan grabbed Jacob's hand and pulled him away from his tiny car. "First of all, we're taking my SUV. I can't fit into that tin can you call a car. Also, if, and I mean if, we" — Dan motioned his hand back and forth between them—"decide to keep these kids, I'm not changing diapers, not feeding, not cleaning them up, or not getting up in the middle of the night. I don't clean up—"he counted off on his fingers—"shit, piss, puke, or snot. Is that clear, Forrest?"

Staring up at Dan without reacting to anything Dan had listed, Jacob said, "Okay, but just what'll you do to help with these precious little ones?"

Dan said smiling, "Just the fun stuff like playing with them, taking them to the zoo, or just playing the big bad bear and chasing them around the house."

Jacob smiled and hugged Dan.

Jacob was on a mission. With him leading the way, they barreled through the store, buying everything from a crib and a toddler bed to clothes, toys, and food. Jacob listened as Dan just grumbled and pushed the cart. He grumbled even more when they needed a second cart. Jacob enlisted two clerks so they could ready things to be delivered to the house within the next hour. Dan pushed one cart and pulled the other. Dan's face lit up when he spotted the *Raggedy Ann and Andy* dolls, and quickly he talked Jacob into buying them. "Come on, Jacob, these dolls are just adorable, one for each one."

Nodding in agreement, Jacob laughed. "I can't wait until BeeBee likes *Barbies*." He beamed at Dan.

Dan stopped. "God, you're so damn gay."

They both burst into laughter.

When they picked out clothes, Dan held up a frilly little pink dress with underpants, socks, and shoes that matched. "Jacob, won't BeeBee be cute in this?"

Someone shouted, "Sheriff, I doubt your ability to fit your big hairy ass in that cutesy little dress."

They turned around to see the city's Chief of Police, Matt Wilder. "Matt, just shut the fuck up, like you don't know what's happening back at my house," Dan groused.

"Hell, yes, I do. I must have had fifty phone calls about how your mother shot through town on two wheels. It took me nearly an hour to track you down. Dan, that woman came close to wiping out half of the town's population! So, Sheriff, just what are you going to do about that?" He huffed at Dan and continued, "And FYI, your deputy, Ricky, is so damned pissed over the fact that you wouldn't let him arrest that mother of yours."

"Her license is pulled until she goes before the judge, and with the reckless driving charge as well as numerous other charges. I'm sure she'll get a big ass fine and lose her license permanently. I hope."

Standing there looking shocked, Jacob snapped, "You're not going to put your wonderful mother through all that! For

God's sake, she just got overly excited."

Dan raised his voice. "Forrest! Don't tell me how to do my job. That woman's a total menace! Her judgment is shaky at best."

Jacob teared up and nodded. "But, Daniel, you're going to break her heart."

Dan's expression changed from dead-serious to a look of total innocence. "Me? Like hell, the judge will do that, not me."

They said their goodbyes to the chief and completed their shopping.

Arriving back home, Dan commented on how many cars were now parked at their home. They found a house full of family. Dan asked the men who'd arrived to help bring in the purchases. Together they all assembled the beds, dressers, and other furniture. They transformed two of the bedrooms into children's nurseries. In short order, everything was complete. Dan walked around complaining and grumbling about all the people in their house, but when he got to the area where the kids were playing, BeeBee stopped and looked up at Dan. Her little cherub face lit up, and she raised her arms to be picked up and squealed, "Dada."

Melting on the spot, Dan went from grumpy to teary-eyed and smiled at her. He scooped that precious baby up and hugged her close. Through tears, he asked Jacob, "God, Forrest, what am I going to do?"

Jacob shrugged and replied, "Love her."

Dan put on his Sheriff Daniel Winters persona. "This family needs bonding time, and y'all need to get the hell out."

Helena confirmed what Dan had stated. "Dan and Jacob are right. Let's give them some time alone."

Dan stopped her. "Aaaah, Mom, you're forbidden to

operate any vehicle until you go before the judge. Mom, are you hearing me?"

Helena smiled. "All this fuss over a little speeding ticket, for heaven's sake."

Dan stayed calm. "You outran a deputy sheriff, and only God, in His wisdom, knows how many other laws you broke. Plus, you nearly gave Dad a heart attack."

Her entire family turned to Helena, and at the same time, they shouted, "Mom!"

Their shocked expression made her step back. "Okay, okay, okay, I got a little overly excited and *maybe* got a tiny bit carried away. I'll just be more careful."

"Like hell, you will. You're not allowed to drive any vehicle until you're arraigned before the judge, and, Mom, he's going to suspend your license. I promise you that. You may even get jail time. I'm not fooling around. No more driving! Mom, this is so God damned serious. They should've arrested you. They didn't arrest you because of me."

She patted his face and gushed, "Thanks for being a good son, and I promise not to drive until I see the judge." She smiled until she saw the expressions on her children's faces. "I just finished saying I wouldn't drive!" She took her husband's arm, and they left, followed by the rest of the family.

One of the smaller nephews tugged on Jacob's pant leg and stage whispered on his way out, "Unco Jacob, you need a naughty word jar. Unco Dan has a potty mouff."

Jacob bent down and kissed his little forehead. "You're so right."

Dan rolled his eyes. "I'm headed for the poor house."

At last, the families all left. Peace and quiet filled their home. RJ and BeeBee sat and played on the floor. Si and Amese, the Siamese cats, took one look at the children and fell in kitty love with them. They bumped foreheads with both little ones, purred for them, kissed them, and threatened Dan if he even walked near them. "Jacob, that has to stop now. If one of your demented cats bites or scratches me, I'm kicking both their asses outside."

Jacob gave that *say-what?* look and replied, "Don't be silly. They're just protecting their babies."

"By taking me out?" Dan barked back. Both cats hissed every time Dan walked near the children, but only until Dan pointed his finger at them and pretended to shoot them. Both cats frantically shot out of the room and down the hall.

Jacob scowled. "What did you do?"

Dan innocently said, "Who me? Nothin."

Jacob told him, "Please play with the kids while I start making us supper."

Dan smiled. "I'm on it." He sat on the floor, then stretched out on his side, propping his head up so he could look at them. "You two are so adorable." He sighed as he stroked RJ's and BeeBee's heads.

The sweet moment lasted for a few minutes when RJ stopped his play and pointed at BeeBee. "Oh no, phewy." Scrunching up his face, he pointed at her again and then pinched his nose closed.

Dan immediately sat up. "You didn't?" he asked BeeBee.

She raised her little arms. "Dada."

"Not a chance, baby girl. You've got a shitty diaper. Holy Moly, I smell you big time."

BeeBee then smiled, clapped her hands, and repeated, "Titty diedie, titty diedie."

Dan shot up and shouted, "Jacob! *Nine-one-one!* We got a *ten-eighteen* here!" He bent down and whispered to BeeBee, "No, say titty diedie, you'll get me in trouble."

Now, even more delighted, she clapped her hands and giggled as she repeated it over and over again.

Jacob flew into the room wide-eyed and panicked. "What is wrong?

The little girl answered, "Titty diedie. Titty diedie."

Jacob's facial expression changed from panicked to pissed off in a split second. "You did not teach her that!" Dan gaped from the baby to Jacob, but he had no words of defense. Jacob bent down and picked BeeBee up. "Oh my, you're a stinky baby." Jacob kissed her little head.

At that moment, RJ chimed in with, "Potty." Then he started doing the potty dance, the one every little boy danced when he needed to go potty and right now.

Jacob flat-out stated, "You have a choice, the baby or RJ."

Dan instantly replied, "Come on, little man."

Jacob shouted after him, "Be sure and clean his bottom when he's finished and clean out the potty chair, too."

Dan moaned. "How in the fu—dge did I get into this shit?"

RJ demanded, "Potty now, Dada!" Dan picked him up and ran.

The *nine-one-one* answered, the *ten-eighteen* got lifted, and the kids were fed and in bed. Dan and Jacob sat on the sofa. Dan pulled Jacob in close. "Forrest, you need to write this down so you remember. I do not do puke, snot, piss, or poop. I do not clean potty chairs or wipe butts."

Jacob sat forward and turned to face Dan. "You did wipe that baby boy's behind, didn't you?"

"That was the first and last kid butt I'll ever wipe."

Jacob just smiled that *you-are-so-wrong* smile.

Within just weeks, Dan and the family gathered for the adoption of RJ and BeeBee. No one objected, so it all happened quickly.

Once the judge sat down, he looked startled when he saw the huge crowd that sat behind Jacob and Dan. BeeBee clung to Dan with all her might, squawking if he even moved to put her down.

RJ, sitting in Jacob's lap, suddenly slapped the table. "Wet's go!" he commanded.

Smiling at the demanding little boy, the judge said, "Yes, little man, let's do that. My, my, this is a huge crowd. Are all of you here for the Winters' adoption?"

They answered with a simple, "Yes."

Again smiling, the judge said to them all, "I've read all the details about how this all occurred. I'm so impressed with this family. All of you joining together to raise these precious children.

"Sheriff Daniel Winters and Dr. Jacob Winters, are you two ready and able to take full custody of these minor children, Belle Bijou and Randal James? Are you willing to bring them into your home as your very own children? Do you understand that they'll be your legal children from this day forward?"

With flowing tears, Dan tried to speak, but in the end, he could only nod.

Jacob answered, "We do, your honor. Sorry, this is such an emotional day for us all."

Finally, gathering in his raw emotions as best as he could, Dan said, "I love these little guys, and I can't imagine life without them in it."

No one held back the happy tears — even the judge quickly wiped a few tears away as he finalized the adoption.

Tyson and Helena insisted that there be an adoption party on the family farm. People from all over came to celebrate this wonderful occasion. BeeBee clapped and cheered, "Dop, dop, dop."

CHAPTER ELEVEN

Just two months later, Jacob was sitting in a meeting with all of the other school administrators. He explained what he'd just learned at the conference with the Department of Education in Atlanta. The changes planned for the entire education system in Georgia proved to be huge. Jacob presented the information and fielded all questions. The members gathered their belongings and thanked Jacob for his hard work and for sharing the important information.

The door to the conference room opened. It was Jacob's secretary. She waved him over to her and said quietly, "Dr. Easton-Winters, there's a policeman here to speak with you. He says it is most urgent." Jacob grabbed his things and followed her out the door. As he was passing the others, he shrugged in confusion.

There stood Officer Blake Pettijohn, who had just joined the force.

Jacob's attention immediately focused on the officer. The young man, looked very pale and spoke with a shaky voice. "Dr. Eaton-Winters, there's been a shooting. Multiple people were injured. Three officers are down, sir. Please come with me, Dr. Easton-Winters, right now. I'll take you to the hospital."

Jacob froze, fear ripping through his entire body. Unable to move or speak, he just stood there.

His secretary, Tina, started to gather the stuff Jacob held and spoke to him, "Dr. Easton-Winters, Are you okay? Now just pull yourself together and find out what's going on! Go on, hurry!"

That snapped Jacob back into reality. "Officer Pettijohn, was Sheriff Winters involved in this? Is he okay?" Jacob questioned as he handed the rest of his stuff to Tina.

"I don't know that information, sir. I was just told to find you and get you to the hospital." Indicating for Jacob to follow him, the officer hurriedly walked through the door with Jacob right behind him.

The two of them got into the car, and just as the door closed, Officer Pettijohn's communicator went off. "Do you have Dr. Winters?"

He responded, "Ten-four, we're on our way!"

Then the dispatcher said, "He's needed there, STAT."

Jacob paled as he heard the word STAT. "God, please let him be okay."

The young officer flipped on the lights and siren. They made it to the hospital in record time. The moment the car stopped, Jacob shot out and ran to the hospital entrance, and Ricky and another officer met him. "Dr. Winters, Sheriff Winters has been shot. The stubborn man refuses any treatment until he speaks to you. We have two other officers that took bullets. One's in surgery now, and the other is about to head there."

Jacob teared up, and there was the sound of panic in his voice. "Ricky, take me to Daniel. Now!"

They headed to the double doors to the ER, but a woman stopped them and flat-out stated, "Sorry, only family members are allowed. I'll need to see some ID."

Jacob's demeanor changed instantly. His face reddened, and his voice became deep and gruff. "My husband, Sheriff Daniel Winters, is back there, and if you don't get the hell out of my way, I'll have this officer arrest you. Move, woman!"

The poor woman dived out of the way in terror.

They ran down the hall toward where other officers stood

outside some drawn curtains. Lieutenant Robert James' face went from concerned to relieved when he saw that Jacob had arrived. "Jacob, he's so fucking stubborn. He took a bullet and has been refusing any treatment until he's sure his officers are okay and until he talked with you."

Jacob's mood went from panicked spouse to strict teacher in an instant.

Reaching his hand out for Jacob, Dan whispered, "Baby, what took you so long to get here? I've got to be sure my officers are okay. Shelly Freed got shot, and she's pregnant, find out if she's okay."

Lieutenant James stepped forward. "Dan, she's fine, and so is the baby. It was only a flesh wound, and she's already out of surgery . . . basically just needed stitches. Kurt's in the OR now, and he's stable. Dan, you need to get that bullet out of your neck right now. This is serious."

Jacob whispered, "How serious?" Robert started to say something when the doctor, a tiny little woman of Asian descent, walked in.

"Mr. Winters, I presume. I'm Dr. Linn. It's very serious! The longer we wait, the more swelling will occur, making the surgery more difficult for me to perform."

Surprised, Jacob said, "Why in the hell haven't we moved on this, then?" All eyes turned to Dan. Jacob rubbed his hand over his face. "Dr. Linn, please get your staff moving. He goes as soon as you're ready." Dr. Linn flew out of the room. With a shaky voice, Jacob said, "Daniel, for God's sake, your goddamn stubbornness is going to kill us both."

Dan took Jacob's hand. "Honey, I love you so much, and if I don't make it—"

Stopping him by covering Dan's mouth, Jacob scolded, "Shut up, you big, dumb ox. I love you, too. That's why you'll make it."

The staff entered in a flurry of activity. Immediately

transferring Dan to a gurney, the team took off.

Still holding Dan's hand, Jacob ran alongside the bed.

They got him to the doors of the OR, and Dr. Linn gave Dan something in the IV. Dan said, "Jacob, I love you."

Then the doctor told Jacob, "He's going to drift out of it now. You can't go any further. So kiss your man and let me do my job." She smiled and squeezed Jacob's other hand. Jacob kissed Dan.

Dan mumbled, "I'll finish this when we get home." His speech slurred, and he went under. Jacob started to cry as he watched them take Daniel away.

Jacob and a couple of officers waited in the waiting room. After an hour, Jacob asked them, "Is anyone minding the shop?"

Ricky, chuckling, answered, "He'd kill us if you were here all alone."

Jacob barked out in laughter. "He would, wouldn't he? I know you all respect and love him, and I promise to keep you updated. I'll be fine. I promise. Go out and protect our community."

A sudden chorus of voices sounded.

"Dad?"

"Uncle Jacob!

"Jacob?"

There stood his sons and niece, and behind them, Daniel's parents. As Jacob stood, his pent-up emotions came to the surface, and he let go. Jacob covered his face and sobbed as his sons and niece engulfed him in a hug.

Helena pushed through, took hold of Jacob, and hugged him hard.

After a few moments, Michael asked, "Dad, how's Pop doing?"

Jacob smiled and touched Michael's beautiful face. "Pop?

Daniel will love that. I don't know yet. He's still in surgery."

Michael smiled and said to him, "He knows, and he got all teared up when we all asked if we could call him that. Our family bulldog, Jovena, will get us an update."

Before Jovena could step toward the reception desk, Dr. Linn blew through the OR doors. "Oh my God, that man of yours! The surgery was easy and smooth. However, I've never known anyone that woke up instantly from anesthesia like your husband. He's pissed because he can't speak, and he won't keep his head still. He wants you, and now."

They entered recovery, and Dan swatted at some nurse.

"Daniel Robert Winters, do I need to call Helena in here? She'll kick your big gorilla butt!"

Dan froze and then reached for Jacob, who hurried over to him, gently caressing his face.

Dr. Linn filled Jacob in on Dan's condition. "He's going to have a very sore throat. Even though the bullet didn't even nick it, I had to push all of that stuff way over to get the bullet. It was lodged against his spine. There appears to be no damage there. However, the more he thrashes around, the more swelling there will be, which could cause damage, even paralysis. So, Sheriff Winters, it would be best if you stayed still. Do you have pain?"

Dan only stared at Jacob.

"Dr. Winters, I'll rely on you to make him follow orders."

Smiling at her and then his husband, Jacob said, "He's putty in my hands."

Dr. Linn chuckled. "I can see that."

In short order, they moved Dan to a private room. He slept for two full days. Jacob went home to check on things and found that a dozen people were watching the kids and tending the animals, which gave Jacob a feeling of great relief. He smiled and through tears, told them, "God Bless you all." then headed right back to the hospital.

Upon returning, Jacob heard Dan's raspy voice in a tirade even before he got to the room. Walking into Dan's room, he was met with, "Where in the hell have you been?"

Jacob turned to Dr. Linn and asked, "How's he doing?"

Dr. Linn responded, "Physically, he's doing well. It's the emotional aspect that concerns me."

Dan was pissed off and hoarsely barked at Jacob, "Tell that woman I'm not crazy. I just need to go home today."

Jacob turned to the doctor, and she laid out the conditions. "If he stays home and out of trouble until his stitches come out, he could go home, but I'm afraid he'll not follow my orders once he's at home."

Jacob took a deep breath and, pointing his finger at Dan, said, "Listen to me, Daniel. Don't ever speak to me like you just did again. Am I clear on that?" Dan blushed with embarrassment and nodded his head. "I'll have them put you in restraints if you don't begin behaving yourself. Now, are you going to go home and behave, or do I leave you here for a couple more days?"

Dan complained, "I want to go home." Dan glanced around Jacob and asked Dr. Linn, "Just how long until I can go back to work?"

Dr. Linn said, "Two weeks." However, she'd been quick to add that he could only do desk work until he fully healed, which would be at least a month.

Dan smiled at Jacob. "Take me home, Forrest. I want to sleep in our bed. Oh yeah. What about sex?"

Dr. Linn deadpanned, "No thanks, I'm spoken for, ba-ha-ha-ha-ha-ha-ha." Dan's facial expression froze her laughter instantly. She blushed deep red, cleared her throat, and replied, "As long as you're careful, there are no restrictions." The cops, who'd just stepped into the room, groaned and quickly headed back out the door.

Dan lit up. "Great, get the hell out, all of you, while I get dressed. Honey, will you help me?" Jacob helped him get ready, and then they sat and waited for the paperwork. Dan fidgeted and complained just a little. But so far, Dan had behaved himself.

The nurse came in with the medical release paperwork and instructions for home care.

When the orderly brought in a wheelchair, Dan sneered at the poor guy and flat-out said, "I'm not riding a fucking wheelchair out of here. Everyone will think I'm too feeble to do my job. I'm walking, and that's final." Dan crossed his arms and glared at everyone.

Jacob quickly cleared things up for Dan. "Fine, you can take the wheelchair back. He'll be staying."

Jacob said to Dan, "You'll just stay here since this is hospital policy, and if you're not ready to follow these simple regulations, then you're not ready to go home."

Dan complained but finally stood up, walked over, and sat in the chair. He stated, "No one takes a picture of me in this chair, and I mean no one! Got it!" His officers quickly nodded.

Jacob smiled. "Yes, Sheriff Winters."

When they arrived home, the little guys scurried into the living room. "Dada. Dada!" little BeeBee called.

RJ chattered away, "Daddy, we miss you so much. Is your booboo hurty? You okay? Did you shoot da bad mans?"

Dan put his hand to his heart, and with a shaky voice, softly said, "The kids missed me."

Jacob replied, "Of course they missed you. They love you."

Then little BeeBee reached out to be picked up. Jacob quickly stepped in and had Dan sit on the sofa, and then he placed their daughter in his lap. "Owweee boos?" she asked, touching his bandage.

Little RJ was on his other side, his brows knitted together and eyes fixed with Dan's. "I thinked you not comed back home." Tears started to form in RJ's eyes as he hugged Dan's arm.

That put Dan over the top with emotions. He coughed, sputtered, and tried to cover his tears. Then the words tumbled out. "Y'all are my family. I'll always come back."

Jacob turned away and covered his face, then a sob burst forth—those words had torn through Jacob and right to his heart.

"Aww, Forrest, not you, too," Dan sputtered with emotion.

Helena stepped into the room and took the children for milk and cookies. Dan stood and moved to where Jacob was standing with his hands covering his face and body shaking. Dan engulfed Jacob in his arms. "Honey, you know you're the most important thing in my life. I love you and our family." Dan held tight and lovingly kissed the top of Jacob's head.

Dan changed into Sheriff Dan. "Wait a minute." Dan then shouted to his mother, "Mom, how in the hell did you get here?"

Jacob took Dan's face in his hands. "Lieutenant Dan, life is a box of—"

Smiling for a second, he cut Jacob off, and with his raspy voice, tried to shout, "Oh no, you don't! She cannot drive . . . period. The judge suspended her license for like . . . forever!"

Jacob took over. "It'll be handled, but not by you. I'm putting you to bed right now. No further discussion. Got it?"

Caving into Jacob's demands, Dan whined. "Forrest, will you lie with me until I go to sleep?"

Jacob smiled. "Of course I will."

Dan recovered quickly and returned to work full-time in less than a month. Despite Jacob's concerns, Dan had obtained a doctor's release and waved it in Jacob's face every time he brought up his concerns.

CHAPTER TWELVE

After hours of discussion with Dan, Jacob decided he no longer desired to work for the school system, especially in his current job. Plus, the State Department's offer looked great. He tended his resignation.

The board took Jacob's resignation badly. He performed his work professionally and went above and beyond his duties, and the board knew that.

Jacob attended a closed session of the board, bringing Dan with him for moral support. The board and school administrators begged Jacob to reconsider his decision to quit.

Dan stood up. "Come on, Jacob, we're out of here."

The board chairman, Josh Martin, pleaded, "Come on, be reasonable."

Dan replied, "Are you kidding me? He should be reasonable? Where were you six assholes when the bitch slandered my husband? When she planted shit in his office? Where were you? You all were hiding behind her! That's where you were! Moreover, you all knew she was a zealot and homophobic. So did you protect your most valuable, tenured, hardworking, dedicated employee? Oh, hell no! You were all too chicken shit to back her down. So no, he's not going to be reasonable at this point. You all can go straight to hell, for all I care."

Josh Martin stood and spoke to Jacob. "Dr. Easton can speak for himself."

Dan's face turned red, and he took two steps toward the man, but Jacob stepped in front of him. He put his hand on Dan's chest and held him back.

"It's Dr. Easton-Winters, and I have no confidence in your abilities to lead this school system. I've given this system thirty years of my life and have an impeccable record and reputation in this county and statewide. You people nearly ruined it. Furthermore, without the assistance of one single person who actually worked in this system, you chose that lazy superintendent, and now you're beginning to realize that it was a huge mistake. You all act like light bulbs just blinked on in your heads, and you've become aware I'm taking my knowledge and leadership abilities with me. Yes, I know this system will struggle without me. But tough!"

Turning to leave, they were stopped by Buck McKenney, a well-known member of the community and new school board member, who stood and spoke. "Jacob, what will it take to keep you here?"

Pausing, Jacob's expression turned to a slight smirk. Dan caught that mischievous grin and nodded encouragement to him. Jacob turned and faced the board. "I want to make one dollar more than the superintendent, and I want forty-five vacation days plus holidays off. I want the superintendent, the chairman of this board, and his cronies to resign. In exchange, I'll drop my lawsuit against this county and stay until a replacement superintendent can be found."

Reacting immediately, Buck flat-out stated, "Done, or at least most of it can be done."

The chairman, his cronies, and the superintendent all stood and shouted, "Not going to happen!"

"No way!"

"You don't have the authority."

At first, Buck just smiled at them, but then he blasted them. "Shut up! All of you! First of all, elections will be here in about two months, and you'll be so humiliated, especially when the lawsuit starts. And as for you, Mr. Superintendent, Dr. Easton-Winters has run our system since before you took the position. You all need to resign before you're forced out or fired." Gathering his belongings, Buck walked to the exit, followed by the other three board members. They waited for Jacob and Dan to leave and then followed them out.

Two days later, notification went out that several school board members and the superintendent had resigned due to personal reasons.

The board formally offered Jacob the job of interim superintendent, and he accepted the position under his terms. Still, he stipulated he would only do it for one year while they found a suitable replacement.

CHAPTER THIRTEEN

Jacob, true to his word, took four weeks off his first summer as superintendent. The school board protested, but Jacob made sure that the assistant superintendent he hired knew what to do.

Jacob's first priorities were his little ones. He took the kids to the pediatrician, with Dan joining him at the clinic. Helping Jacob unbuckle the children, Dan picked up BeeBee while Jacob took RJ. Both kids had wide eyes and frightened looks as they walked into the office.

Jacob signed them in, and the nurse escorted them to the examining room.

Sitting down and both kids clinging tightly to them, Dan whispered to Jacob, "Do we have to do this?"

Looking at Dan, Jacob whispered back, "So are you willing to risk the health of our kids so they won't cry a little? Now who's the big baby?"

The doctor walked into the room before Dan answered.

"Okay, gentlemen, I'm Dr. Morris Gerndalson. I've searched and found the few records available for Randal and Belle. So we need to start the vaccination process for both children right away. They'll need a series of shots. The nurse will set up a schedule."

Daniel turned a bit pale and cuddled BeeBee to his chest.

Dr. Gerndalson said, "We'll start with the baby. Let's put her on the table in case we need to hold her down some."

Jacob's eyes widened in surprise, and then his face morphed into an angry scowl. "That'll not happen. We'll hold them ourselves while you administer the vaccines."

Dr. Gerndalson balked at that idea and then tried a more authoritative attitude. "It has been our experience that it's best if parents let us do our job and not interfere with the process."

Jacob and Dan both bristled at the same time, but Jacob spoke first. "Let me clue you in, doctor. Your procedures are archaic, barbaric, and cruel. I've been through this before, and even back thirty-some years ago, good pediatricians abandoned your methods of manhandling infants and children." Jacob stood, and Dan followed. "We need to find a doctor who knows what he or she's doing and one who understands and adapts to each child's needs. Let's go, Daniel." Jacob, Dan, and the kids exited the examination room.

Dr. Gerndalson decided to be abrasive. "You'll still be charged for this office visit."

Dan stopped dead in his tracks—he turned, puffed up, and stood very tall. "You wanna bet on that, doc? I wonder if the American Board of Pediatrics would agree with any of your methods?" They left without any further comment.

As they walked out the door, the nurse whispered to Jacob, "Go to Dr. Carlene Wilson. She's the best."

As the door to the clinic closed, Dan stood still a moment just outside and listened. He heard the nurse as she yelled at the doctor, "Are you a complete idiot? That was Sheriff Winters and his husband, Dr. Easton-Winters, Superintendent of Schools. Damn, I'm going to have to find a new job!"

Dan started chuckling, making BeeBee giggle, too.

Looking at Dan and their baby girl, Jacob asked, "What on earth has you two so tickled?"

Dan answered, "Nothing."

Baby BeeBee hiding her face against Dan's neck, said, "No ting."

Giving them both a lifted-eyebrow look, Jacob responded,

"Yeah, right."

That nurse had given them such great advice. Dr. Wilson earned the title of Saint among Baby Doctors. Little RJ hardly knew he even got one shot, let alone two. BeeBee, however, howled like a wolf and sobbed in Dan's arms.

Noticing that Dan got all teary-eyed, Jacob chided, "God, you're such a wuss."

Dan sniffed it up and then whined back, "She's my baby."

Walking to Dan's SUV, Jacob loaded RJ and waited for Dan to load BeeBee. Getting her all set, Dan walked around and helped Jacob get in.

BeeBee milked her perceived pain and suffering out the door, into the car, and still milked it most of the way home.

She said over and over to Dan, "Owweee, Dada. Bad dodo, bad dodo, poked my weg."

She continued until Dan suggested, "Maybe some ice cream will make it better?" The crying magically disappeared, and both kids cheered.

"You know she's the boss, right?" Jacob asked.

Dan smiled and responded, "Yep, just like her grandma."

Jacob said, quite seriously, "Just imagine this, your mother living with us twenty-four seven for the next eighteen years."

Dan sat quietly for a few moments, then he turned and looked directly at Jacob, his only reply was, "Crap."

EPILOGUE

Dan and Jacob watched as the families gathered around the giant Christmas tree they'd put up in the living room.

Several weeks prior, Dan had taken their two little ones and his brothers' kids to shop for a tree. BeeBee seemed to know just what she wanted, and every time the group picked out a tree, she said, "No, no wike it." Dan realized they were about to run out of choices. BeeBee suddenly lit up and pointed. "Dat one." It was enormous but gorgeous. Dan looked at the kids, and they nodded their heads in agreement.

"Then that's the one we'll get," Dan told the group.

Dan and the kids tried and tried to get the tree into the house, Jacob laughed until he cried watching. RJ carried the naughty word jar around and kept telling Dan, "Bad word, put a dollar in the jar!"

"Forrest, get on the phone and get my brothers here before we need to mortgage the house to pay off that fu . . . stupid bad word jar."

The brothers came, and the tree was cut and shaped to fit perfectly in the house.

Two days later, the families gathered to decorate it. Under the direction and orders of Helena and Jovena, the outcome was spectacular.

For the next couple of days, every time someone put a new present under the tree, BeeBee squealed, "*Mine!*" They had to put a kid gate to the living room to keep her out and prevent her from ripping open every present under the tree.

On Christmas Eve, the family gathered for caroling and the

opening of presents. Dan and Jacob sat with BeeBee between them so she would focus only on the gifts before her and not attempt to open everyone else's. Gramma and Grampa Winters helped little RJ with his.

"Nuf bad singing, *prwesents!*" RJ announced, and all the kids chimed in agreement.

So the chaos began, presents ripped open and aahed over, the giver thanked and on to the next one. BeeBee was not so anxious to move on after opening a present. She had to be encouraged to keep opening. She would squeal with delight and want to stop everything to play with the new toy or put on her new clothes. RJ was the same. The adults gently prodded them to move to the next gift.

Every present was an exciting new experience for all the children. That was until BeeBee opened her gift from Gramma Helena. She tore open the wrapping and looked into the box. She froze for a second, and then let out a blood-curdling scream. She climbed onto Dan and hung on for dear life.

Puzzled, Jacob tipped the box to examine the contents. What he saw caused his head to pop back in surprise. His face said it all.

Dan grabbed the box, looked in it, and barked, "Good God, what the hell's that? It looks like a dead baby. Ma, what were you thinking?"

Dan picked up the box and showed everyone what was inside, "Look, everyone, it's Baby Embalmed.

"*Ewwww!*" Filled the room.

Helena just huffed. "It looks just like the most adorable, sleeping baby." Taking another look at it, she admitted, "Okay, now that you mention it, it's kind of creepy."

"Icky baby, icky baby," BeeBee said over and over, not daring to even look at it. Jacob picked it up and moved it into the kitchen, out of sight. BeeBee went back to her old self now. She let go of Dan, walked over to the shelf, and got the naughty word jar. She brought it to Dan. "Dolla!" she demanded.

Dan rifled through his pocket and brought out a five. Bee-Bee snatched it and put it in the jar. Shaking her little finger at Dan, she said, "Bad Dada!"

Jacob asked Dan, "Do you know what scares me the most?"

"No, honey, what?" Dan responded.

"That she knows all the naughty words. Now, where and how did she learn that?" Jacob scolded.

All eyes turned to Dan.

Dan opened his mouth, but nothing came out. His entire face reddened, and then he rubbed it with his hand, covering it for a second. "I need to work on that."

It was time for church, and the crowd got ready and loaded the vehicles. Dan asked Helena and Tyson, Sr. to load the children. He then said to Jacob, "Hold on a minute. I've something special for you."

Dan hurried to the hall closet, got at a wrapped present, and handed it to Jacob. Jacob tore it open. It was a picture of Dan, Jovena, Jason, Kato, TY Jr., Michael, BeeBee, and RJ, all dressed up. Dan thought it was so perfect.

Jacob placed the picture on the mantle without a word, stepped back, and looked at it.

"Don't you like it?" Dan asked as he gently put his hands on Jacob's shoulders.

Jacob turned, tears trickled down his cheeks, and Forrest answered, "Lieutenant Dan, it's the most special gift I've ever received."

"Damn, Forrest, I love you." Dan pulled Jacob into his arms and kissed him.

"*Wet's go!*" Bossy little BeeBee ended that moment. Jacob's laughter broke the kiss, and off to church they went.

With church over and everyone in bed asleep, Dan stepped

into their bedroom where Jacob sat thinking. His dreamy look and gentle smile showed nothing but total contentment. Seeing his face, Dan asked, "Forrest, just what are you daydreaming about?"

Jacob's eyes drifted to Dan, and he spoke softly and dreamily. "About how wonderful it all is and how I probably would've been alone here in this bedroom tonight, if I hadn't met my Lieutenant Dan."

Tears blurred Dan's eyes as he pulled Jacob into his arms, and with his deep sexy voice, he said, "We filled each other's life. I'm so glad I have you, Forrest."

Jacob reached and grabbed a wrapped present from the nightstand and handed it to Dan.

"I love you, too, Lieutenant Dan." Jacob hugged Dan's neck.

Dan ripped open the paper. It was a box of chocolates.

About the Author

I am a retired educator living on a farm in the northeast Georgia Mountains. I spend time writing and tending the many animals on the farm. I live with my teenage son and Papa.